THE WIN

REBELS OF RIDGECREST HIGH #4

BELLE HARPER

CHAPTER 1
JACE

When shit hits the fan, I can always rely on Hunter to keep a level head.

Roman's quiet and unpredictable. When something goes down, he switches to fight mode. He has for as long as I can remember.

I'm more than happy to run my mouth. I lose myself, drowning in my thoughts, before unleashing an anger that explodes over everything I touch. It's something I need to work on. I haven't always been like this.

But Hunter. He always thinks rationally, analyzing and thinking things through. Makes a small joke to keep me grounded. Holds Roman's fight at bay long enough to figure things out. Or just stands by our sides when we need him and the fight is inevitable.

Over the years, this is just how we've been. I've

relied on Hunter to always keep it together. To be the one in control.

But as I watch his fists fly, his mouth spewing anger, I realize he's only able to keep it together for so long. I've seen him fight. Hell, we've had our fair share of fistfights. But this is a side of Hunter I've never seen before.

It scares me.

If he's lost, then what hope do I have of keeping the darkness at bay? What hope do we have of stopping Roman from losing it completely? From sinking back into that dark place that took him from us when Mila first left. One that we worked so hard to get him out of. But he never fully came back to us until Mila returned.

I can't do this again. The only person who can help isn't here and is the reason this is going down. *Fuck.*

"Stop," I yell at Hunter.

He looks at me, his eyes dark and full of sadness. I feel for him. Fuck, I feel the same way. He pauses for a split second, watching me, before turning back and slamming his fist into Asher's mouth. *Fuck.* I have to stop this. Need to be the one with the level head. I have to keep us together while Mila's not here.

I rush over and grab Hunter, shoving him back before he takes another swing. Asher scrambles back, trying to get away, bleeding from a gash on the side of his head. His eyes are wild, full of hurt and misery, the same as the rest of us. We all feel this way right now, and it breaks my heart to know this isn't something we can just go fix for our girl.

One fucking day.

That's all it took for Hunter to flip and go after Asher. We found out what happened with Mila from Asher. He told us about her stepdad—how she's been taken into custody—and we rushed over here as soon as we could.

Only, I thought we were here to talk about what to do next. How we can help her. But as soon as Hunter saw the look on Asher's face, he lost it, unleashing hell on Mila's almost-stepbrother. And Asher took it, not fighting back. Which only angered Hunter more.

Hunter lets out a strangled scream as Roman holds him back. He bucks and thrashes, but Roman doesn't let him go, just standing there and taking it all as Hunter slowly wears himself out. Until he's barely standing and Roman's holding him up.

"I'm sorry, Hunter."

I turn to see Asher. His eyes are full of unshed tears, and I shake my head. He doesn't need to be sorry. This isn't his fault... Well, it partially is. But I can't blame him for that. God, when Mila is finally mine, I'll do the same. Only, I won't be stupid enough to get caught.

"Let me go, Roman. I'm gonna fucking kill him."

Hunter's voice is hoarse from all the screaming he's done in the past ten minutes.

He's trying everything he can to get out from Roman's grip again, and I release a deep breath and run my hands through my hair. "Fuck. Hunter, just give it up," I call out to him, and he stills.

His eyes are still on Asher, but I can see the hurt now. He hates fighting; he's the one to kill someone with love rather than fists. And I know he's going to feel guilty for what he did to Asher and then will spiral hard. Roman lets him go, and Hunter stumbles a little.

I reach my hand down to Asher, who eyes me wearily for a moment before taking it. As I help him off his front lawn, I can't help but think the neighbors must be having a field day with this drama. Thank god James and Kate aren't here. They're on their way to New York for Mila.

"Thanks." Asher nods at me and I grit my teeth.

Don't get me wrong—I want to slam my fist into his mouth just as much as Hunter. But I know Mila wouldn't approve of me beating up her boyfriend, especially since I'm still not one of them. Not officially, anyway. I want to be in her good graces when she comes home. I'm not going to let her get away with toying with me anymore.

She will be mine.

I know she didn't kill her stepfather. She hates her mom, not him. She told me he wasn't a bad guy. Just dumb for marrying her mom. I don't give a shit what the news is broadcasting; I know she wouldn't have. It's just a matter of time until they find who did and let her go so she can come home.

Bending down, I pick Hunter's glasses up off the lawn. He didn't take the time to put in his contacts, since he rushed over here as soon as Asher called us and just laid into him.

Hunter takes his glasses from me with a small, "Thanks," and puts them on. He lets out a deep breath. I place my hand on his shoulder and he sags under my touch.

"I'm done." He looks over to Asher then drops his head. The fight has left him and been replaced with guilt.

Roman holds his other shoulder, and we all just stand there, breathing deeply and letting Hunter know that it's okay. We're not upset with him; we understand. Blood trickles out from where Asher's holding the gash against his temple. Head wounds always bleed more, so it looks worse than it is.

I move from Hunter to Asher and hold his shoulder, giving it a small squeeze. "Come on. Let's get you cleaned up and work out what we are gonna do about Mila." I nod my head toward his house, and he nods.

Roman and Hunter follow us to the house. Madison's standing in the front door, her hand over her mouth and tears streaming down her face. Fuck, the sight of her hits me right in the chest.

She shouldn't have seen that. I know Hunter won't react well to knowing she did, and I don't need him to completely zone out on us today.

"It's okay. It's over now. That won't happen again." I look back at Hunter, and his face pales at the sight of Madison.

He shakes his head. "I'm sorry, Madison."

Madison nods, wrapping her arms around herself tightly, and sniffs. Asher smiles at her, but the blood trickling down the side of his face and onto his tee has her letting out a small sob.

"It's okay, Mads. I'm fine. Just a minor cut." Asher opens his arms to her, and she hesitates.

Watching Hunter from the corner of my eye, I can see in his expression he's disappointed in the way he reacted. But he's still here with us.

He scared me, but from Madison's point of view, it would have been much worse. She had to watch the one person left here to protect her getting attacked by someone who's supposed to have his back.

Madison goes to Asher, and he wraps his arms tightly around her.

Hunter clears his throat. "I'm sorry, Madison," Hunter whispers now. The guilt is going to eat him up.

She gives him a tight-lipped smile and whispers, "It's okay."

"It's not okay, but I'll make it up to you."

She looks at me from her brother's arms, and I nod for her to come help me, reaching my hand out for her to take. She pulls away from Asher a little, and he gently pushes her toward me. I can see she doesn't want to be away from him, but I take her hand and squeeze it gently.

Turning to Roman, I ask, "Can you find a towel and get him cleaned up? We will find something to patch that up." I point to Asher's head and Roman nods.

Looking down at Madison, I give her my best smile, the one that makes all the girls weak at the knees. I know I shouldn't use it on her, but I need to see her smile. I don't want her to tell James and Kate what happened. That's the last thing they need, especially if they tell Mila.

Luckily, Madison smiles back at me, blinking up at me under her wet lashes. I might not have a winning personality, but my smile sure does.

"Mads, can you show me where your mom keeps all the medical stuff? We will have him right as rain in no time."

Her eyes widen at my use of her nickname, and she nods.

"Then we will order pizza, all pile into the living room, watch movies, and wait together. We won't leave until your mom or James is back, okay? We'll stay with you."

Wiping her nose with the back of her hand, she sniffs. "Promise?" she croaks out. She's so small now beside me. Since she's only three years younger, I never think too much about her age, but those years show right now.

Fuck. This poor girl. Caught up in all this shit. I pull her to my side, wrapping my arm around her shoulder. "I promise. Mila's my girl. You're her sister. I'll take care of you until they come back."

She gives me a watery smile. "Mila will come back."

God, I hope she's right.

CHAPTER 2
MILA

've always said my mom is an actress. Only, I didn't know how good she really was until now.

Malcolm's barely been gone, and she's acting like nothing's changed at all. At home, she's been her usual self. She ordered a new Versace handbag, booked a trip to the salon, and called her interior designer and asked her to come by to update the apartment.

The very same apartment Malcolm was alive in mere days ago. The one we're in now, after the police finished their investigation. That room—the guest bedroom—is no longer being used. It's where all my nightmares start each night, only to wake up and see the blood on my hands.

How could I have killed him and not remember a thing?

The doctors told me I blocked out the incident

and that Mom's in shock. That's why she's behaving like Malcolm is going to come home at any moment. That she believes he is. I know better. She's fake. Everything about her is, right down to the French manicure she got this morning while the police interrogated me. Our lawyer told us not to speak to the media, that we need to keep quiet to help with my case.

On the television screen in front of me is the sad widow on the news, sobbing into her Kleenex. Completely different to the person I'm living with off-screen. Like she cares whether speaking to the press will ruin my case. Being in the spotlight is what she loves the most. She has no heart; she only cares about herself, and the rest of us are just pawns in her game. Just what that game is, I don't yet know. But I'm going to find out.

"It's been so hard for me and our baby. She will never know her father." Mom holds her freshly manicured nails over her rounded belly.

I roll my eyes when the reporters fall for it and tell her how sorry they are for her loss. Is it a loss to her? Really? Malcom's bank account seems to be working well enough for her, and the only thing she's lost is an old man she married for money.

"I will never know love like Malcolm again."

My stomach turns at the lie.

For her performance on the screen, she deserves an Oscar. She doesn't care he's gone. She only married him for the money, and now that he's dead, she's a rich woman and loving it. She can't even wait until he's in the ground to lap up all the attention. I feel sorry for Malcolm, falling into this viper's trap.

"How are you feeling after finding your daughter had murdered Malcolm?"

My breath catches in my throat. *Fuck...* don't answer them. Please don't say a thing, Mom. This is why you're not supposed to speak to the press. It will only make things harder on me. *Please don't answer, Mom.*

"It was very hard walking in and finding her holding the bloody knife and his lifeless body there. I will never get that image from my mind." She lets out a fake sob as my body sinks to the floor.

I drop my face into my hands and cry. Why? Why would she say that? Unless she *wants* me to go down for this murder...

It's been a week. One entire week since I woke up with blood on my hands, and I can't get the memory of Malcolm's eyes from my mind. I haven't slept. Every time I do, I have nightmares. I've barely eaten, and I just want to go home... back to Kate's house. I'll even stop seeing Asher until I'm eighteen if that's what they want. I just don't want to be here anymore.

My dad and Kate have been here for me all week.

They are my only support, even if I can barely see them. Mom doesn't care what happens to me. She only cares about all the money she's just inherited. I wonder how she got Malcolm to screw over his own child and leave him nothing.

I've been asking where Junior is. He was here that night, but I haven't seen him since. I never liked the guy, but I don't want something bad to happen to him, either. Like, this was his dad. That's gotta be hard news to take. He has a drug problem; I just hope he hasn't done any harm to himself.

His own mother can't even find him. She has been by every day, looking for him, and I feel sorry for Gail when we have to tell her we haven't seen him. The cops want to question him about that night, but even they can't seem to locate him. Someone needs to be looking after him right now. This isn't the time for him to be alone.

Dad and Kate have been working with the lawyer Mom hired to help me. I know I didn't kill him... I wasn't even awake. This lawyer doesn't believe me. He seems to think I'm wasting time by not admitting to killing Malcolm. That he can get me a deal if I admit to it. He wants to get the charges lessened from murder to manslaughter so I don't end up with a life sentence.

I will not admit to something I didn't do. *I didn't kill him.* The only people who believe me here are Dad and Kate.

Dad can't afford another lawyer for me; I wouldn't even ask him. But Kate has suggested helping find another one. I know she doesn't have the money for that. Her ex-husband doesn't even give her any child support. I overheard that conversation with my dad when they were talking about how much they would need for a lawyer. It made me sad to know that asshole doesn't see his kids and doesn't pay for them, either.

I said I was fine; I don't need another lawyer. That it's a misunderstanding and the truth will come out. Only, it's not... It's not getting better.

And I'm not fine.

I'm barely holding on here. I don't trust anyone and anything they say. My phone might be bugged. By my mom? The cops? I don't know, I just can't take the chance. So the only messages I have sent to the guys is that I love them. They clued on fast and sent the same in return after blowing up my phone with questions on that first day. The day Malcolm died, it was on the news, *everywhere.*

The press has labeled me a killer. *A monster.*

The cops have questioned me many times about the sexual abuse my mother told them about. Asking if that's the motive behind my killing Malcolm. I've told them repeatedly, until my voice was hoarse, and my eyes couldn't see through the tears, that I didn't kill him. That he never abused me. *Not once.*

He was good to me, but that's not good enough

for them. It's not what they want to hear. They want me to confess to killing him, to get it off my chest. Live without the guilt.

The only guilt I have is not telling my dad about Asher and me. If he'd known about us, he wouldn't have sent me back here. Malcolm would still be alive... At least, I hope he would be.

But once again, I'm locked in a room with my lawyer, George Batten, an old and graying man. He's the worst lawyer I've ever met. I swear, Mom found him on Craigslist and is paying him peanuts. He wears an outdated, ill-fitting suit, and his briefcase is falling apart.

He can't even organize his own paperwork. It all slips out every time he opens the case, and he can never find mine. He never interjects when the cops ask me questions they shouldn't; he just sits there and watches the clock. Probably counting how many peanuts he gets before going back to the circus.

I'm at the station with the same two cops who've interrogated me from the start: Officer Holliday, a middle-aged, balding guy, and Officer Andrews, a brunette woman in her thirties. She told me to call her by her first name, Grace. As if we were going to be best friends and I'd spill the beans to her in a "girl talk" session. She has tried girl talk multiple times. But I'm not dumb; I see what game she's playing. My mom plays it too. Only, she's much better at it.

Right now, I'm going over what happened that

night and morning, again. Same story, over and over. Nothing new or different since nothing else has changed.

"Malcolm wanted me to come back. He said something happened and wanted me to come back for a few days. I assumed it had to do with Mom and the baby." I don't mention that, when he'd called, I'd said no to returning and told him she's not my mother.

"With Junior there that night, I thought maybe he wanted to tell us they were getting a divorce. They didn't look happy. He appeared... somber. Mom seemed like she was trying to delay things, but Malcolm wanted us to sit down to talk. But I had a headache from crying over what happened back home with Dad. I don't remember a thing after I sat on that couch."

"So, you were angry at your dad, and you took it out on Malcolm."

I grip the sides of my head and take a deep breath to stop myself from screaming at him. Holliday has been chasing this story for a week. He nods as he scribbles something on his notepad.

"No. Why don't you listen to me?" I know why— because it looks like I killed him. From the outside looking in, I would think so too. But there is much more to this story, I just know it.

"That's not the truth, and we know it, Mila. Let's not dance around this again today. Let's get this guilt that's eating at you. I can see how much it's affecting you; you've lost weight. Tell us the truth. That you killed Malcolm. His blood is on your hands."

I look down to my shaking hands... Blood. Thick, red blood coated them while the cops trained their guns on me. My ears rang, and I didn't understand what was happening. I was groggy... so tired. Even now, I hear the voice of my mother telling them not to shoot me. That it was self-defense.

Why would I have killed him? No matter how many times I play it over in my head, I can't understand how I ended up there.

I had no defensive wounds, no cuts on my hands, and no marks on my body at all. Yet, I had killed a grown man with a knife? Someone had stabbed him multiple times. There were defensive wounds. He had tried to fend off his attacker. He could have easily fought me off; I'm five-five on a good day, and he was at least six-three and had a hundred pounds on me.

I was wearing the same outfit I walked off the plane with. I didn't change; I just went to bed? In the guest room? Not even my bedroom. But how did I get there? My mother wouldn't have been able to carry me, but Malcolm could have. Did he attack me? And I killed him? But where did I get a knife from? I would have had to go to the kitchen and get one, come back and stab him, and somehow fight him off without getting one mark on me.

All these questions have been asked... *by me.* But there are no answers. The officers just stare at me like I should tell them how it all happened. Like I have the answers and am just trying to delay things.

The cops believe I did it, and to anyone on the outside, it would look like that. I had the knife in my hand, his blood on my hands, and his body beside me. They just want me to say I did it and charge me. Close the case and move on. I know, because I overheard them talking about it. How they can't just let me get away with saying it was self-defense. I already killed a man back home with a knife in self-defense and got away with it. Only, I didn't, and I can't tell them that. *I'm not a killer.*

Why would I have a knife in my room? Unless it was premeditated.

"Mila, it's okay. This is a safe space," Grace says. "Tell us why you killed Malcolm, what really happened, and we'll understand. We get it. He abused you, and it was more than you could take, so you did what you had to to stop him. Then we can all go home and have a shower."

The only reason I get to go home is because my mom always keeps up the self-defense argument, and I'm in her custody. At least I don't have to stay here in a cell.

Fake therapist Grace is at it again. Putting stories out there and hoping I'll cave from the pressure of being in here for hours and finally tell them I did it. I look from her to Holliday and his bald patch. He plays his bad cop to her good cop; maybe he should get an Oscar with my mother.

"You can't deny you were holding the knife. That you were covered in his blood, and he was lying on your bed beside you. The evidence doesn't lie, Mila. Your mother called nine-one-one as soon as she saw what had happened. She feared for her own life."

Feared for her own life? *The hell.*

I let out a deep, shuddering breath and sag into the chair. I don't speak, and I don't look at them. Anything I say will be turned against me. My lawyer just shifts his weight on his chair, and I internally roll my eyes at him. Useless prick.

"Do you want us to play the tape of her call? You can hear how scared she is. It might help you remember what really happened," Grace suggests.

Do I want to hear it? Of course, I do. It's the best thing they've offered all day.

"Yes," I grit out between my teeth, because I know there's more to this story than what Mom said, and she has to know what really happened. She won't talk to me about it, she doesn't want to be caught in a lie herself. But I will catch her... it's just a matter of time.

As I pull my sleeves down over my hands, I tuck my knees to my chest and rest my cheek on them. I want to go home. I want to hug my boys. God, it hurts so bad to think about them. It's like a stab to the chest that I might never get to see them again.

I wait as they start the tape. The hairs on my arms raise as I hear her voice, that dramatic wailing that is obviously an act. How can they not hear that?

"Come, hurry, my husband tried to attack my daughter, and she killed him. I need help."

I shake my head but listen as the operator explains how to give CPR to Malcolm, and she's telling them I'm holding the knife at her, so she can't get in the room to help him.

"I'm scared she might kill me if I try help to him. Please hurry. I'm pregnant and scared." There's a muffled sound and then she says, "Put down the knife." *Beep.* "It's okay. You're safe now, Mila."

I sit up taller and listen more closely and hear a beep again.

That's the sound the refrigerator makes when the door is left open too long. And who stands in front of the fridge too long?

Junior.

"Go back." I sit up and point at the table. "She isn't in the room. She's in the kitchen. Listen to the beep in the background."

Officer Holliday's eyes narrow, and he sits back a little, crossing his arms over his chest. But Grace gives a puzzled expression and nods, reaching for the recording. I let out a deep breath. She believes me. At least it's a step in the right direction.

"Go back just a little bit. You will hear it. The beep warning you to close the door. Junior stands in front of the refrigerator all the time, and it beeps. Malcolm was always yelling at him to close the door."

Holliday just points at me with a sly smile. "Ah, good try. Junior wasn't there."

"Yes, he was." I swear to god. What is this guy smoking? "Malcolm Junior was there when I got to the apartment. That's what I've said from the start. You never listen."

He shifts in his chair, making himself look bigger, and I run my hands through my lifeless hair.

"So, you're saying Junior was at the apartment when you got there, but he wasn't when you killed your stepfather?" Grace tilts her head, and I know she wants me to say yes… Yes, he was there and yes, I killed Malcolm. Sly bitch. I'm tired as all hell, but not that tired.

"All I remember about when I got to the apartment is the headache, Mom giving me something for it, and sitting down beside Junior. Malcolm said he had a headache as well, and Mom got him something. Then just waking up in the room with everything."

"So, you both had a headache, and your mom got you what? Advil?"

I look up at Grace and shake my head. "She didn't have any. She gave me two white pills." I freeze as a shiver runs down my spine.

I knew my mom didn't like me... but she could never. She wouldn't. Not her own daughter. I look up at Grace. *Holy shit*. The reason I fell asleep so fast finally makes sense. I was exhausted already, but I never just pass out like that.

"She drugged me."

She drugged me, and then she framed me.

CHAPTER 3
ROMAN

"Give me the car," I yell at Hunter for the tenth time today. I can't sit back here and wait any longer. He shakes his head, his fist balled as if he's going to hit me.

"No, you're not going. We'll stay here and wait until it's the right time. We don't want to make things worse for her."

"Fuck this," I spit out. Being there will not make things worse. But me not being with her will... I can't stand this. I can't be away from her any longer.

I need her like I need air. I can't breathe without her, and it feels like I've been holding my breath for two agonizing weeks.

I need to touch her, hold her in my arms and keep her safe. She needs me as much as I need her.

I growl lowly in warning. "I'm not waiting anymore. You said she would be back for Christmas.

You say that us being here is the right move; it's not. She's all alone, Hunter. She needs us... I need her."

I'm shaking, I can't go back to that place. That dark hole I know will eat me whole this time. There will be no coming back from there. I know it, and I think Hunter does too.

"I know," he says. "I need her too. You don't think I want to be there with her? Without her, I feel lost."

Fuck. I need to stop taking this out on him. I know I'm not the only one in this relationship, and I have to think about my brother. Hunter's my family too, and I didn't think about how he's struggling.

"I can't take it anymore. Something's going on, and James not being able to really see or talk to her... that's not good."

Hunter's father told us not to go to New York. Said that it would only cause trouble for Mila and us because of my father's death. But if it means having Mila home and safe, I'll go to the cops and tell them I did it. I'm the one who killed my father, not Mila. They will have to let her go.

I will spend the rest of my life in prison to keep her out of it. What happens to me isn't important. I only care that she's safe.

"I thought she would be back." Hunter's shoulders sag as he drops onto the sofa.

I shouldn't have yelled at him like that; I'm just so worked up. Without her, I can't sleep, and I'm not functioning. Going to him, I reach for his shoulder and squeeze it.

I'm getting better at physical touch with Hunter. I don't flinch away anymore when he touches me, and I can offer him the comfort of my touch, even if it's just his shoulder. He looks up at me and gives me a small smile as he looks to my hand.

"Sorry. I shouldn't have blamed you. We all thought she'd be back."

We did. I don't think James and Kate expected that she would still be there. Kate came back and James stayed. We thought the cops would let her come back home here, but she has to stay with her mom.

"There's no way she killed him. She had no motive. These cops are just incompetent."

Except, who's gonna believe her? The press has been calling her the killer stepdaughter, saying she killed him for his money. Only, she wasn't in his will; she will inherit nothing. But her slimy mother inherits everything.

There's just so many things wrong with that bitch, pointing to her being the actual killer. Mila said she didn't do it, and I know she didn't. She just needs someone there for her… I need her.

"I need to go to her now." Need to feel her in my arms, need to protect her and be with her. Even if it's to hold her at night while she sleeps.

"No, man. Just give it another week, and she'll be back."

He won't even look at me because he's lying. He doesn't have the answers this time. I can see it's tearing him apart. What is his father holding over his head if he leaves? There has to be more to it than him wanting to protect Mila by staying here.

Hunter's always so with it; he's the one who keeps us all together. The glue. But now, he's lost his way. I don't know if anyone can help him but Mila. He needs her as much as I do. And I will bring her back for him.

I throw my hands up, and without a word, I storm out of the house to my Harley. I've contemplated riding it to New York, but the snow and ice that I'll encounter on my journey has been the only thing stopping me. Never experienced snow before, but the first time I do, I don't want to be on two wheels.

The engine vibrates underneath me as I rev it a few times before tearing out of the driveway and toward Jace's house. It's Grady who greets me. He's closing his car door when he sees me, and smiling, he waves over at me.

"Roman, how have you been?" Then his smile drops and he shake his head. "Sorry, dumb question."

I shrug. Not a dumb question. If it were any other

day, Mila would still be here with us. "I'm here for Jace," I let him know.

Grady nods toward the front door, and I follow after him. His parents are home, and I nod hello to Daniel in the living room. Ella rushes to me from the kitchen and hugs me. Grady pauses and raises his arm to stop her, knowing I don't like to be touched. He's one of the few other people who's ever picked up on that, but I hug his mom back, welcoming the warmth and love from her. She's always been like a mother to me.

"Jace is in his bedroom, Roman. He hasn't been out in days. Maybe you can help him? Talk to him?"

I nod. But I know how he feels. I feel the same way, not wanting to get up to face another day without her here. Unable to help her. But we can't just lie down and let her be taken from us like this. We have to fight for her, and he's going to do that by giving me his car.

I stomp up the stairs two at a time and don't even knock as I slam his bedroom door open. He jumps up in bed, spinning his head to me. It's dark in here, and it smells like he hasn't showered in days. I can see he's naked as he uses his sheet to cover his junk.

When his eyes meet mine, they're bloodshot, and he rubs away tears from his cheek. I wasn't expecting that. I don't think I've ever seen him cry. I take a step back. This isn't what I'd been expecting when I came up here.

"The fuck, man? Don't you fucking knock?" he croaks as he sits taller, and I see his chest more clearly. He looks like he's lost a few pounds.

"Have you not been eating?"

With a shrug, he reaches for his phone. When finds no messages, just like I did this morning, he slams his phone down and lets out a pained groan.

"You can't stop eating. You need to take care of yourself for Mila. She'll be stressed out if she sees that you've lost weight. Then she will give you all the hugs, and I'll have to steal her from you."

He rolls his eyes, flops back down on his pillow, and twists to look up at me. He quirks his brow, and I can see a hint of a smile. "You've been living with Hunter too long. You're sounding like him."

I shrug. He chuckles, but the humor doesn't meet his eyes.

"Yeah, and he's acting like me. That's why I need to bring her back."

I've never seen Hunter lose his cool before, not like he did with Asher. Fuck, I haven't seen Asher since then. I now fear he will look just like Jace, and I can't be worrying about them all right now. I need to get Mila back.

"I'm here to get your car keys."

He raises a brow at me. "I thought Hunter said you couldn't go."

I grunt and Jace just chuckles. This time, it does

reach his eyes, and I know once Mila's back, he will be just fine.

He points to his dresser, where the keys sit in plain sight. "Just so you know, if he asks, I didn't give them to you. I'm gonna say you stole them."

I don't care what he says, because it won't matter when I have Mila back with us. I place the key to my Harley on his dresser, and Jace shakes his head. He has no idea how to ride it, so he'll have to get a lift with Grady.

I sweep his keys into my fist and walk out the door, turning back to him before I close it. "I'll bring her back. So, have a shower and eat a sandwich. Because I'm getting all the hugs."

He laughs. "Is that a bet?" he calls as I close the door.

"Game on," I reply before I turn and meet Grady at the top of the stairs.

He holds something in his hand. "It's a long drive, and gas isn't cheap."

I hesitate. He's giving me cash. *Fuck.* I didn't think about that. I don't have a lot to my name. Normally, I wouldn't accept it; I never want to be treated like a charity case.

But this isn't a normal situation.

"For Mila." He pushes the money into my hand. "You will get her back. I know you will."

I nod, emotions I'm not used to bubbling up. As I step forward, Grady's brows quirk, and I reach an arm around and pat him on the back a few times. It's awkward and weird and I don't think I'm doing it right. But then his arm comes up and gently pats my back.

He smiles, and I grunt as I pull away, no longer wanting to talk about what just happened. But it felt… nice. He's always been like a big brother to me, so it felt… right.

CHAPTER 4
ROMAN

I've been driving for sixteen hours straight. It's over forty hours to get to the apartment building where Mila's staying. I stop off at a gas station, fill up, take a leak, and stock up on snacks and energy drinks. I'm not stopping until I'm halfway there.

Even then, I'll find a truck stop, take a shower, and sleep a few hours before taking off again. I want to be kissing her for New Year's, and I don't have much time left.

Hunter's been blowing up my phone, but I haven't answered any of his calls. I can't deal with that right now, since he will know what I'm doing by now. Jace will have told him. I don't want him to try and talk me out of it.

I glance down at the clock in the car; it's 3:44 a.m., and I can barely see straight. When I open the window to wake up, the cold air hits me, and I shiver. I know I'm getting close to snow, and I need to keep my wits about me.

Spotting the lights of a truck stop up ahead, I let out a deep breath. My body is stiff and sore from being stuck in the same position for so long. I'm not halfway, like I wanted to be, but if I take a quick nap, I'll be good to go in a few hours. I pull in and find a place to park until then.

Thank god I didn't take my Harley, since I would have had to stay in a motel. Jace's car is pretty big, and if I drop the back seat down, I should be able to sleep fairly comfortably. Only, in my haste, I forgot to bring a blanket or a pillow with me. I didn't even pack a change of clothes. But it doesn't matter. I can get something when I'm in New York.

Thirty hours later, and I'm in New York. I feel hot and wired from too many gas station coffees and energy drinks. My ass went numb about five hours ago, and I don't think I will ever feel it again.

The city's huge. So much bigger than I'd seen in photos and on TV shows. I drove through a lot of cities to get here, and each time I thought they were huge, but nothing compares to New York City.

A car honks, a taxi driver yells. There are people everywhere. They don't even care that you're trying to drive; they just walk right in front of the car like they don't care about their life. I'm worried that I've made it all the way here just to hit a pedestrian and end up in jail before I even get a chance to see Mila.

I've never left Ridgecrest. Not in the same sense other people do. We moved to the trailer park when I was six, from one a couple of towns over. So, I've lived in the same place my whole life. Hell, the short trip to Alessandro Amato's place is the farthest I'd ever been away from Ridgecrest.

Until now.

I already hate the city. Too many people, too many cars. I've never felt claustrophobic in my whole life until today. I look down at my phone's GPS—just a few more streets, a few more turns, and I'll be outside her apartment building.

Someone bangs on the hood of Jace's car and screams, "Watch where you're going."

My knuckles turn white on the steering wheel as I grip it tight. I want to get out and hit this fucker. But I'm so close to Mila. I have to hold it in.

I look out my window and up at the tall building as I approach it. Fuck.

There's nowhere to park the car, and I spot a news crew standing, waiting in the front. Fucking slimy bastards trying to get a story. The only story is that Mila's innocent, and I'm here to bring her back home.

Turning down an alleyway, I find nothing but no parking signs; where am I supposed to park in this city? I give up. I've been driving for too long, I'm exhausted, and I just need to hold Mila in my arms.

I park and jump out of the car, and the instant chill in the air has me wrapping my arms across my chest. When I left, I knew there would be snow, but I didn't even think to bring a jacket. Okay... I don't really have one. Not one for snow, at least.

After locking the car, I head toward the building. I know she lives in the penthouse. It's like that story of Rapunzel. Mila's all the way up in the tower, and I've come to rescue her.

I shove past the press and, seeing the doorman busy trying to push them back, slip into the rotating door of the building. The lobby's huge, and the man behind the desk raises his head at my approach. But I don't need, or want, to talk to him. I know what floor she's on.

As I walk over to the elevators, the sound of my boots on the marble floor echoes around the otherwise quiet lobby. But before I can push the button, the man behind the desk appears and stops me by grabbing my arm.

"Excuse me. Can I help you?"

I shake his hand off my arm. "No." Don't need this guy's help. "Know where I'm going," I mumble. I'm tired and wired at the same time and so close to my girl. I don't want trouble. I just need to get up to her.

"Are you here to see someone?" he asks, standing

in front of me and blocking me from going any farther.

I take a step back and look him up and down. He's an older guy with graying hair, wearing a black penguin suit. I see a hint of a tattoo under his shirt collar, so he's not a complete suit. I grit my teeth and relax my hands. I can't make a scene here; the press is watching.

"I'm here to see my girlfriend. Mila Hart. She lives in the penthouse."

His cold blue eyes narrow at me. My hands flex into fists, but other than a slight tick in his jaw, he doesn't react.

"You're not on the list."

What fucking list? "I don't need to be on a list. I'm her boyfriend."

He looks down at my tattoos, at my jeans I've been wearing for almost three days, and the lack of proper clothes for New York in winter.

The man jerks his head to come over to his desk, and I begrudgingly follow him. He isn't going to let me up if I don't. After picking up a black receiver, he dials a number. He better not call the cops. I've done nothing but come to see my girlfriend, and there are no rules against that.

I guess I should have told Mila I was coming. But I wanted this to be a surprise.

"Hello, Mary… Yes." He smiles. "I have a visitor

down here for Mila Hart, but she has no visitors on the list."

Can't even have visitors? Her mother has gone too far.

"Yes, her boyfriend." He looks at me. "Yes... of course." He smiles again.

He looks up at me, and his smile drops. Fuck. His eyes are judging me, but I don't give a shit what he sees. If I can't get up there to see Mila, I will find another way.

"What's your name, kid?"

I cross my arms over my chest and eye him down. "Roman Valentine."

He repeats my name back to the person on the other end of the line. It better not be her mom—she would never agree to let me come up. She never approved of me when we were kids.

"Not a problem. Thanks again." He hangs up the phone and looks up at me.

I can't read his face as he keeps me waiting for a few moments longer.

"Okay, kid. Apparently, Mila forgot to put you on the list. She's out right now, but the housekeeper, Mary, said you can come up and wait."

I let out a small sigh of relief. She's not there, but she will be, and she's going to be so surprised when she sees me.

He looks me over once again and gives me a small smile. "Mila's a splendid girl. Always sweet to me. You treat her right, you hear me? She needs all the support she can get right now."

I nod, not knowing what to say in response.

He looks at my empty hands. "Do you have any bags with you?"

I shake my head.

"You've never been to New York before, have you?"

I raise my brow at him. Obviously, I look out of place wearing a tee when it's been snowing out there.

"I can show you where to go if you want some warmer clothes."

Is he trying to get rid of me? "I'm good," I gruffly say as I walk over to the elevator, ignoring him as best I can.

"If you change your mind, I'll be here till nine."

I don't reply, and the elevator doors glide open almost as soon as I press the call button. Inside, I select the floor labeled only PH. I've never been up that high before, and my stomach lurches on the ride up. I don't know how people do this every day. I feel sick.

The doors don't open right away, and I begin to panic that the elevator is broken. But then it beeps, and the doors slide apart.

Stepping out, I find myself in a huge open space and freeze. This place looks like an art gallery. It's too perfect and impersonal for anyone to live here. There are white marble floors throughout, a huge, dark kitchen, and a black leather couch over a white rug in the living room. Sunlight streams in through floor-to-ceiling windows, and I can see the tops of skyscrapers from where I stand.

My stomach lurches at how high I am. Fuck. Do I have a thing about heights now?

"Hello, you must be the famous Roman. I'm Mary."

I turn to find a middle-aged woman wearing a blue uniform dress looking up at me and clear my throat. "Yes."

She grins even more. As I look around to see if anyone else is here, I feel her take my hand. I flinch away slightly, and she just pats my arm. "No one else is here, dear. Just you and me. But I've heard everything about you."

I can't help but smile at that. Mila's been telling this woman all about me.

"She told me you're the shy one who doesn't say very much, but when you do, it's always meaningful."

I like that Mila's taken the time to describe me to this woman. And she's remembered. "It's hard to get a word in when Mila's around," I reply.

Mary laughs, nodding her head. "Oh, well, we know the same Mila Hart." She beams up at me as she pulls me toward the kitchen. She pats a stool and I take a seat. Rounding the counter, she turns her back to me and opens the refrigerator. "Would you like some orange juice? A sandwich?"

When she turns to look at me, my stomach chooses that moment to rumble, and she chuckles. I nod shyly at her now. I should have eaten more on the way here. Not all that junk.

"Let's get you fed, then you can tell me all about yourself." I purse my lips and she laughs again. "Just joking. I know you don't talk much, and I've already heard everything about you."

I raise my brow... How much has Mila told her?

"When Mila first came here years ago, she used to tell me all about her best friends back home. But she talked about you the most. I'm so glad she got to go back home and that everything worked out between you. She really needs you. Needs *all* of you."

I wonder if she knows about us all... Hunter, Asher, and Jace. Or if she thinks they're just her friends.

"I'm here to take her home. I'm not leaving without her."

Mary places a sandwich and a glass of orange juice in front of me. Then she places her hand on top of mine. I don't flinch away this time; I feel comfortable with her already. Mila obviously trusts her enough to tell her about me.

"Are the others coming?" She gives me a small smile.

I shake my head. "They were told to wait for her to come back."

She cocks her brow. "But not you?"

I grunt but don't answer.

She pats my hand. "Oh, I think you'll be my favorite of her boyfriends."

This time, my smile reaches my eyes. I take a bite of the sandwich and almost moan at how good it is.

I like her.

CHAPTER 5
MILA

t has been a long day. All I want to do is crawl in my bed and cry. I try to be strong, but I can only go on for so long.

I arrive in the apartment with Mom trailing behind me. She hasn't spoken to me since she picked me up from the police station. I have nothing I want to say to her right now, anyway. It's not like she's going to admit what she did. But now that I know what she's capable of, I don't want to live here anymore. I fear what she might do to me.

I just want to live with my dad. But until the current custody order is overruled, staying here is my only option. I can't even leave the building alone.

The smell of roast lamb hits me as I walk into the kitchen. Mary's fixing her famous roast dinner. I want to kiss her; she knows how much I love her roasts. She smiles over at me and opens her mouth to say something, but Mom butts in.

"Oh, Mary. I forgot you were here," Mom says in a tone that says she believes Mary is beneath her.

I hate the way she speaks to her... Mom used to serve. She was a flight attendant once. She should know how it feels to be talked down to, but now that she has all the money in the world, she's above everyone. Including me.

Mom throws her bag on the coffee table and turns to the both of us as she taps away on her phone with a clicking of her nails. I hate that sound.

Eventually, she looks up at us. "I'm going out for dinner with some friends. I won't be back tonight." She eyes me, and I know she will have security downstairs to stop me leaving. I know because I've already tried.

I want to scream at her. I want to tell her I know she's the killer... that I'm going to prove that she killed Malcolm. But while I'm still here, I need to be careful. I can't say these things, or she will kill me. I just know it.

She lets out a small huff when I don't respond. What am I supposed to say? Have a great night? I'll be locked up here in the penthouse, crying myself to sleep, like I do every night.

My mom turns off toward her room, leaving me alone with Mary. She's not a grieving widow tonight.

I hope the press sees her and questions what the hell she's doing out with her friends so soon after the death of her beloved husband.

Hell, maybe I should ask her where she's going and tip them off.

Mary clears her throat, and I turn to find her smiling at me. It's the first time I've seen her smile since I've been back.

"Mila, why don't you go to your room and freshen up? I left you something in there." She beams at me with a twinkle in her eye.

"A gift?" I ask, and she nods and pushes me toward my room.

"A gift. I left it on your bed." She winks at me and puts her finger to her lips. I take a deep breath and nod. I have to be quiet about it. She's trying to cheer me up; it's sweet, but nothing's going to make this day any better. Even chocolate.

"Yeah, a shower's a great idea. I need to wash this day off me."

The one thing I'm grateful for is that my room is the same as I left it, which is strange. I thought my mother would have turned it into something else already. I'd been gone six months, but she left my room untouched.

There are enough rooms in this apartment, and she's already turned one into a nursery for the baby. It's a beautiful nursery; she must've had the designer help her with it, because god only knows, my mother doesn't have that kind of taste.

I make my way to my room, which is as far away from my mom's as possible. Opening the door, I close it behind me with a soft click. I flick the light switch and gasp, my hand going to my throat when I see the figure on my bed.

I watch as he sits up. "Roman?"

He's been sleeping… on my bed. In New York. He's here with me. How? When? I can't form words; I'm too overwhelmed with emotions.

"Mila," he says with a sleepy voice.

I choke out a sob—he's real. He's really here in my room.

He rushes over and wraps me in his large arms, and I smell him. The smell is like home. Roman's here. He came for me. *I knew he would.*

I burst into tears, and he rubs my back without saying a word. How did he get here? Did he fly? How did he even get into the building?

Then I realize it was Mary. This is my gift, the reason she's smiling so big out there. She knows all about my guys. I've told her all about Roman over the years, and she would have known who he was right away and let him up.

"Oh god, I missed you so much." I didn't realize how much I needed him here until now.

"I've missed you," he whispers as he places a kiss on my head.

I pull back and look up at him. He looks exhausted. Like he hasn't slept in days. "Did you drive all the way here?" He smiles down at me and nods. "Alone?" His smile drops, and he nods again. I shake my head and kiss him. He drove all the way here for me.

"How are the others? I couldn't really talk to any of you. I'm pretty sure my phone is bugged by my mom and I don't want anybody else getting in trouble for things in the past."

I didn't want them to mention Roman's dad or how he'd died. I don't need to worry about them getting into trouble because we're not being careful.

He grunts. "We guessed as much." He twirls strands of my hair in his fingers and kisses me again, and I melt into his arms.

"Mom will kick you out if she finds you here."

He shrugs, not seeming worried. But I am. I can't have him here only for her to take him away from me.

"Mary likes me. She told me all about myself." He raises a brow and I chuckle.

Oh god, what did she tell him? All the stuff I love about him, probably. Jace… I don't know if Mary would have let him up. I smile to myself; no, she would have let him up. I told her all the nice things he's done for me since he got done being an asshole.

"How have you been?" he asks, and I can't hold back.

I cry again, and he leads me down to the bed, wraps me in his arms, and holds me as I let out everything I've been holding inside.

There's a knock at the door. I sit up, look over at Roman, and back at the door. Fuck, it's my mom. I scramble up, and Roman does the same until we hear, "It's just me, dears. We're all alone, and I have dinner ready for you. Come out whenever you're ready. I'll be off until morning. Have a good night, lovebirds."

I let out a deep breath as my shoulders drop. "Thank you, Mary," I call out to her. "And thank you for the gift in my room. If it wasn't for you, he wouldn't have been allowed up here."

Her responding chuckle is audible from the other side of the door. "You deserved a very handsome gift, Mila."

I giggle. "He's the most handsome gift I've ever received."

Roman's cheeks turn a shade of pink. I poke his arm, and he shakes his head. Oh, my big bad Roman is all embarrassed now.

"It's our little secret," Mary says. "Don't worry about your mom. I'll keep him here unnoticed." And with that, she leaves.

Roman being here will have to be our secret.

Mom wouldn't allow him here; she's isolating me from everyone. I bet it's her plan to drive me crazy. Only, she doesn't know the cops are now onto her... thanks to that beep. That one small sound was all Grace needed to question things more. She cut the interview short and left with some other officers. But I don't want to think about that now; I just want to be happy for a few hours and not think about anything that's been happening.

"I need a shower." I groan.

I don't want to get up off the bed. I'm worried that if I let go of Roman and take a shower, he won't be here when I come back. That this will turn out to be only a dream. If this is a dream, I don't wanna wake up, don't wanna face the reality of tomorrow alone.

"Go have a shower. I'll wait for you here." He must read it on my face as he brushes his fingers over my cheek and tilts his head. "Want me to come wash your hair?" He pushes my hair behind my ear and cups my jaw. Bringing his lips to mine, he kisses me lightly.

My hand slides up and tangles with his hair, and I deepen the kiss. No matter how many times I kiss Roman, he makes my toes curl. When he pulls away, I try to chase his kiss, and he chuckles. He gestures toward the bathroom with his eyes, and I shake my head and smile. I don't feel like a shower now.

"Let's get you cleaned up." The smirk on his face tells me I'll be getting a little dirty first.

I grab a fist of his T-shirt and drag him across the bed with me. He comes willingly. I walk backward, not taking my eyes off him for even a second. He smiles down at me, then takes the back of my neck in his hand and pulls me to his lips and kisses me so hard, I feel it all the way to my toes.

He pulls away, his eyes boring deep into mine. "I'm not going anywhere, Mila."

My heart explodes with all the love I have for this man. "I love you, Roman Valentine. You're mine. Always and forever."

His mouth crushes to mine, and when I gasp, his tongue slides in. The taste of him has me intoxicated, wanting more.

I break the kiss for only a moment to pull up his T-shirt. He takes the hint and, in one swift movement, it's over his head and on the floor. My chest rises in anticipation as he grabs the hem to my hoodie and takes it and my tee off, leaving me standing there in my blue lace bra and jeans.

His finger skims along the sensitive skin of my throat. Traces along the lace cup of my bra then trails down over my belly button and hooks inside the waistband of my jeans. He tugs, and my body falls into his, my hands going to his chest. Roman grunts in pleasure. He welcomes my touch... like it's a drug and he can't wait to get his next fix. At least that's how I feel when I'm with him.

He lifts his hands to the sides of my face, brushing my hair back. Looking deep into my eyes, he says, "I love you, Mila Hart. I always have and I always will."

My body wants to show him just how badly I want him, and my soul longs to prove how much I love him. I reach for his jeans and pop the button open, followed by the zipper. Sliding my hand past the waistband and into his boxers, I find his hard velvet cock and wrap my fingers around the thick length. He groans into my mouth as his hips flex into my fist. I stroke him, and he grows harder to my touch. He fucks my fist, moaning but never breaking his kiss from me.

He suddenly breaks away from my mouth to let out a guttural moan. "Fuck, Mila." He holds my wrist to stop me from stroking him more, and I smirk up at him.

I watch as he tries to slow down; he must have been close. He looks down at me with those blue eyes, and I bite my lower lip as I grip him tighter.

His eyes widen as he lets out a shuddering breath. "Fuck, Mila. I want to be in you when I come. I want us to come together."

My mouth drops open. Just hearing those words has me rubbing my thighs together. I need to be touched.

Roman might not be a man of many words, but that was before... He's come a long way from the boy I once knew. The boy who pushed Hunter and Jace in the schoolyard and waited for me to hug him. I loved him back then, but the love I have for him now is so much bigger. I love the man that he is now.

But fuck... he's been listening to Hunter's dirty mouth. Not going to complain.

I reach up and grab his hair, pulling his face to mine and kissing him. I give him everything I can in that kiss, showing him how much I love him and how much I want him.

He flicks open my jeans, and I shimmy out of them until I'm standing there in my lace thong and bra. He takes a step back, and I try to follow him, but he puts his hand out to stop me.

His eyes roam my body, and I suck in a breath at the sight of fresh ink on his chest. I have no idea how I missed that when I took his shirt off. I guess I'd been a little preoccupied with something else. But my hand reaches out and goes to my name on his chest. The script is beautiful, and it blends in well with the other tattoos there... the daisy I drew him beside it.

I trace my finger along the letters. "Roman," I whisper, holding back tears and trying to swallow the lump in my throat.

"I got it the day you left." I let out a small sob, and he shakes his head. "Don't cry. I didn't want to make you cry."

"I wasn't leaving you. I never wanted to leave."

Roman wraps his arms around me in an embrace, his warm body hard against mine. He smiles down at me, holding my hand now in his large one. "I know you weren't leaving me, Mila. I wanted to wear your name. So everyone knows you belong to me." He growls, and I feel it all the way to my core.

"I never got my tattoo," I say with a pout.

His eyes growing darker, he wraps his hand around my throat, and my eyes widen. "I know exactly where I want to put it." He slaps my ass, and I jump with a small yelp. He uses that to spin me around. My back is now flush with his front, and I can see us in the mirror. His erection rubs against my lower back.

His hand stays on my throat as his other traces down my body and under my thong. I let out a moan as his fingers slide through my already wet folds. His fingers find my clit, and he flicks it with his thumb. Pleasure throbs through me, and my hips buck into his hand. But his hand around my throat never moves. It holds me. I'm pinned against him. And I love it.

One of my hands reaches back for his thigh and the other holds the crook of his arm as he strokes me slowly, never taking his eyes from me in the mirror. Just watching him doing this to me turns me on. I'm so close; I just need a little more. His fingers move down to my entrance, and he dips one in and rubs against that sweet spot inside me.

"Roman," I gasp.

He pulls his finger out of me, and I whimper at the loss, but then he's back on my clit. The guy is playing my body. He remembers every little sound and move I make and knows how to get me off every time.

He keeps up the pace on my bundle of nerves, knowing when to ease the pressure and when to give me more until I'm arching my back and silently screaming my release as he continues to strum my clit, prolonging the orgasm until I can't take anymore. Now that I'm oversensitive and wrung out, he lets up.

I look up to see him in the mirror, his eyes on mine as he sucks his fingers and licks off my arousal. My core clenches with the need for him to be inside me.

He peels his fingers from my throat, and I move toward the counter, dropping my thong and removing my bra. Placing my hands on the counter, I arch my back, exposing myself to him. He groans at my display, reaching into his jeans and pulling out his thick cock.

He strokes himself a few times before dropping the rest of his clothes and standing naked behind me. His body is a work of art. All the tattoos… the abs.

The scars he wears on the outside are his past. My name on his chest… that's his future.

If I can prove I didn't kill Malcolm.

I don't want to think about what will happen if I end up behind bars for this. Roman needs me. And god, I need him so much right now.

His hand rests on my lower back as he lines up his dick with my entrance. I feel him nudge against me, and my eyes meet his in the mirror. He grips my hip and slides in.

"Roman." I gasp his name as he sinks all the way in. His eyes never leave mine as he pumps, in and out. Slowly. Then he smacks my ass cheek before slamming deep into me, and I gasp, my legs shaking at the pleasure.

He smacks the other ass cheek and slams into me again, and I find it hard to stand. "Holy shit," I pant as he watches me.

Roman repeats the moves over and over until he grunts his release, and I tumble over the edge with him. His fingers dig into my hips as he releases inside of me, and I call his name. When his fingers find my clit, I call out again as I ride out another orgasm.

My arms shake with the strain of holding myself against the counter, but Roman doesn't pull out of me. He leans over, wrapping his arm under my chest and over my shoulder, pulling me back so I'm flush against his chest with his cock still nestled inside me.

He brushes his thumb over my nipple and whispers into my ear, "We need to fuck in front of the mirror more. That was hot to watch."

My mouth drops open as my core throbs against his cock, and he groans.

Fuck... my boy has me speechless after only a few words.

CHAPTER 6
ROMAN

New Year's Eve in New York City.

This should be an exciting time. It's one of those special occasions that people travel to the city for. Only, I have spent most of the day locked in Mila's bedroom while she's interrogated by the cops, trying to work out how I can help her from here.

When she returns to the apartment, she looks exhausted. She's not the same Mila who grew up with us, and she's not the same Mila who returned home six months ago, either. Then, she was grown up and just as bossy.

This Mila, she's withdrawing. Pulling away from us... from me. As if she already knows how this is all going to end. But I won't give up. I'll never give up on her. I spent the day looking over all the news articles to see what the press believes went down. I read all the nasty comments people left, but I was only looking for the ones with theories about what happened.

Divorce and affair… Those two were thrown around a lot. That Mila was having an affair with Malcolm and killed him in a fit of jealousy. Or that Amber—her mother—killed him because she was jealous of her daughter and blamed Mila for his death. That Amber had an affair and the baby isn't Malcolm's. That Malcolm was divorcing her, and Mila killed him for her mother, since she inherited everything.

So many different theories, but there are people out there who don't think Mila killed him. I'm working with those theories. One might be closer to the truth than the story that's currently circulating. I can work out a way to help her, to clear her name.

"Mom's gone," Mila says. "I'm hoping you'd like to spend New Year's with me on the rooftop in the courtyard?"

I squeeze her hand in mine and pull her in for a kiss. I want her to forget about the day and have a good time. I want to have a special evening with her, and no better time than New Year's. "That sounds amazing."

Okay, it didn't, but when her smile grew wider, I knew it was the right response. I've decided that, yes, I have a thing about heights. Mary invited me out of the bedroom for some lunch earlier, and I couldn't look out the windows. It gave me vertigo and I felt sick.

She'd told me, *"You won't fall out. You can run at them, and they won't shatter."*

I'd told her, *"That's okay, I don't need a demonstration."*

She'd chuckled and replied, *"I wouldn't have dreamed of doing it."* But the twinkle in her eye told me she might just to mess with me.

Mary's nice. I like her. I wish she'd been Mila's mom. She takes care of her here, not Amber.

"I packed a blanket and some yummy snacks. Mary got us a couple of beers." Her eyebrows wiggle at me, and I chuckle, because Mary had asked me earlier what alcohol I would drink on New Year's if I'd been twenty-one. I told her beer. No specific kind, just beer.

Mary must have gone out and got us a couple while I'd been hiding in the bedroom, trying to work out what Amber's motive was for killing her husband. Apart from the money. Was he really trying to divorce her? Mila seemed to think so. So, I'd been working on that angle.

"Are you trying to get me drunk, Mila?" I tease her and she snorts, but I can see her grin.

"You caught me. I'm trying to have my wicked way with you."

I pull her body to mine, letting her feel the bulge in my jeans. "You can do all the wicked things, anytime you want. No need for beer." She playfully slaps my chest, and I'm smiling, glad the darkness in her eyes is gone. At least for now. I will chase her demons away for her. *Always*.

"We can do the wicked things at midnight, after you kiss me." She leads me to the elevator, and I'm confused. I thought there weren't any more buttons to take us up to the rooftop. But she stops outside a door and pulls out a key. I thought it was a coat closet, but when she unlocks and opens the door, I see it contains stairs leading up to the rooftop. The chilly air hits us, and I remember now that I only have a T-shirt and jeans on. I don't know how long I can stay out there. Mila's still wearing the coat she had on today.

"Shit, I forgot about how cold it was. Hold on, and I will grab you a jacket."

I want to protest; I don't want her borrowing her dead stepfather's coat. That seems weird to me.

She returns and hands me a gray puffer jacket. "I stole it from Junior. He's smaller than you, but it should fit."

It's better than the alternative—going out there in a T-shirt. I never would have worn Malcolm's clothes.

I push my arms through the sleeves and it's snug. Junior must have skinny arms because I'm struggling to get it on over my biceps. When I finally get my other arm out, I look down and Mila giggles.

"Maybe we need to get you a scarf to cover this." She runs her hands down my chest where the jacket won't meet.

I shake my head. "I'll just hold you in my arms and that'll be all the warmth I need." And it's true. She's all I need to keep warm out there, because I won't be letting her go. Because I love her and also a little part of me is worried she may blow away out there.

Okay, this heights thing is really getting to me. I need to stop thinking like that. She'll be fine. Unless there's a gust of wind. Fuck. My heart races, and I'm sending myself into a panic over nothing. That can't happen.

She holds my hand and leads me up the stairs covered in a fine dusting of snow and into the night air. I look up at the sky and take a deep breath. It's impossible to see the stars, but they're up there above us. We are so much closer to them now. But the clouds are thick and threatening to dump snow on us. I've watched it from inside today, safely away from the windows.

But I haven't actually been in the snow before, and I really hope it snows tonight. Not much, just enough to make this night magical for Mila.

I look around the area and find that this little courtyard must belong to the penthouse Mila lives in. It's surrounded by a large wall, and there's a garden with some small shrubs, fake grass, and a little seating area with wrought iron furniture. Mila ignores the love seat and pulls me into the middle of the fake grass and lays down the blanket she brought up.

I help straighten it out before I sit down, opening my legs wide and reaching for her to come sit between them. She places the bag of food and beers beside us and sits between my legs, leaning back into me. I feel rather than hear her sigh.

"This is exactly where I want to be on New Year's." I wrap my arms around her and hold her against me.

I feel a little guilty that I get to share this moment with her while the others are back home, worried about her. I text Hunter earlier and let him know I'm here. That Mila needs us, and I wasn't wrong in coming. He replied with, *"Take care of our girl and I will do everything I can from here."*

"Do you want to video call the guys?" I ask. My phone won't be bugged, and I think it's safe out here. If they bugged the apartment, then the cops know I'm here, and they haven't come looking for me to see if I know anything. So I would say we're safe to use my phone.

She turns in my arms and gives me a sad smile. "Can we? Not that I don't love you being here. It's just, I miss them all so much."

I kiss her little pink nose, and it's cold to the touch. "Even Jace?" I ask, wondering when she will stop messing with him. Not that I don't find that funny as all hell. I love the way she shit-stirs him and he gets all crazy and worked up.

She chuckles. "Even Jace. Being here has made me realize how much I love him. And how I wish I'd kissed him before I left."

I pull my phone out, and Mila *tsks* at the screen. "Hey, if you're not nice to my phone, you can't use it." I'm teasing her, but I just want to see her smile again.

She takes it from me, and I can see her smile in the glass's reflection before the screensaver lights up. It's a photo of us. My hair is in braids and I'm wearing my football gear. Her hair is down and she's smiling at the camera. I'm looking down at her.

"I love that photo of us, but you need a new screen. How does it even work with that many cracks in it?"

I chuckle. "It's bad, but it works."

I unlock it, not hiding the password from her. If she ever needs my phone, she will need to know it. I have nothing to hide in there. She can look at all my photos and read any messages she wants. I know she won't, though; she knows how big trust is between us all. And I would hide nothing from her. If she wants to know, I will tell her.

Pulling up the "boyfriend" chat, I press the camera button and it dials.

"You guys have your own chat? Without me?" She sounds sad.

I didn't think that would bother her. I need to keep in touch with the guys, especially after what happened here. We couldn't bring her into the chat.

"Only since you've been here. So we can all keep in contact and let each other know what's happening."

She nods. "I think it's cute you called it 'boyfriends.'"

I chuckle. "That was Jace's idea. He started it and named it that."

She turns to me and raises her brow at me. Oh man. I know that look. She's gonna mess with him. And if it makes her smile, then I'm all for it. I just hope Jace is. Last time I saw him, he was all kinds of fucked up.

Asher's the first to come on the screen; his hair's a mess and he's not wearing a shirt. He coughs when he sees Mila on the screen waving at him. He's eating something. I forget he's three hours behind, which means it's only about six there.

"Mila." He coughs again, and then the phone is yanked away and Madison and Kate replace him behind the camera. Madison lets out a small sob and waves to Mila. I feel her tense under me; I didn't want crying. This was supposed to be happy.

"Asher, are you okay?" She brings the phone

closer to her face, as if she'll be able to see past Kate and Madison.

"Hi, love." Kate waves as I hear Asher coughing loudly.

"Is Asher okay?" she asks again. I'm worried about him too; I think he inhaled his dinner.

"He was just surprised to see you." Kate smiles and Mila relaxes.

They chat, and Madison joins in when she's stopped crying. Jace has picked up the call but not Hunter. Jace drops out not long after, and I feel Mila deflate.

"He's just gonna get Hunter," I whisper into her hair, and she nods and continues chatting with Madison again.

I rest my head on her shoulder and watch the two of them animatedly talk about some TV series they're watching. Something with vampires. Apparently, they're hot, and I find out they don't sparkle when I ask.

When Kate came back from New York, she made us all get together at her place. She fed us and told us she accepts the relationship we all have. She doesn't understand it, but she loves Asher and Mila. And if we are all going to love Mila, then we all need to be on the same page.

Easier said than done when Hunter already messed up Asher's face. But I think that's what prompted the meeting. She made Hunter and me take home meals she'd cooked. We told her we were fine, but she insisted and told us to call her if we need anything. Even if it's a ride to the doctor or to buy a new pair of shoes.

I think Mila must have told her Hunter and I are living alone in that big house, and Kate wanted to take care of us. While Mila's gone, at least. I hope she's still sending meals to Hunter.

"Hi, Roman." Kate waves at me.

I wave back. I like her. She's a great mom, like Ella. It makes me miss my mom.

"I dropped by Hunter's yesterday and gave him some pasta."

I smile and nod at her. I hope he ate it.

Hunter finally appears, and Jace joins right after. Hunter calls out to Mila, and she sobs, not able to get a word out. Kate and Madison wave and hand the phone back to Asher, who is walking to another room so we can all talk privately.

"Hey, Mila," Jace says, and she sobs again.

I take the phone from her hand while she wipes her face. Their faces are full of worry. "She's good, guys," I tell them. "She's just missing you all."

They all talk at once, saying how much they miss her, and she giggles and sniffs.

"I miss you all too." She wipes her eyes again and holds my hand with the phone.

"Roman, my parents are a little mad at you," Jace says.

Why? Because I took his car?

"Can't you read signs, fucker? My car got towed… in New York City."

"Fuck," I mutter. I shouldn't have parked there. I knew it, but I needed to get to Mila.

"Roman." She turns to me. "Where did you park?"

I shake my head. That doesn't matter. "It was worth it. I'll get it out for you," I let him know. "Say sorry to Daniel and Ella for me. It's hard to find a parking space around here."

"We have a parking garage in the building, Roman. You should have told me. I just assumed you parked in there."

"No worries. I'll get it out," Hunter tells me. But this isn't about me. This is for Mila.

They all start talking over each other, and she laughs. "You know, this is so much harder than I thought it would be."

And they all stop.

"Asher," I call out and he smiles.

"Mila, I'm so sorry. We should have waited. Told my mom, at least."

She shakes her head. "No, I couldn't wait. I know we should have, but it's okay. Really, I was asked to come back here regardless, and I know I could have only put it off for so long. It's not your fault. So, please don't blame yourself."

I know how torn up he is over it all. Hell, I know

he won't stop blaming himself for a long time. It would take me a lifetime to forgive myself for that.

"I love you," he tells her, and she shifts between my legs.

"I love you too, Asher."

"Okay, Hunter," I say.

I see Jace's face fall slightly, but I know Hunter needs to go next.

"Hey, babe. I miss you." His smile never meets his eyes, and I wish it would. The dark circles under his eyes tell me he's still not been sleeping. I know how hard it is right now at his home. His dad's not around, and his mom's been gone for a while. I don't know if she's even coming back.

But if I get Mila back home, at least I know I can get that smile of his back. His jokes and all. I miss that; I miss my friend. My brother.

"I miss you too, Hunter. Have you been looking after yourself?" she asks.

Fuck, she can see how bad he is through my shitty screen.

He nods. "Yeah, Kate gave me some pasta. Are you going to watch the fireworks?" he asks, and she nods.

"Yeah, do you all want to watch with us?"

I look at my phone, and I only have twenty-three percent left on the battery. Fuck, I should have charged it.

Before they can answer, I quickly speak up. "I

didn't charge my phone during the day, so we might need to call you all back for that." No way my phone will last three hours with them all on there.

"Jace," I call out. He's been moving around and waiting his turn.

"Hey, beautiful," he says.

She tilts her head and sighs. "Hey, handsome. I wish I'd kissed you before I left."

He grins. "You can kiss me when you get back." She almost deflates at that, and he notices. "I'll show you exactly where you can kiss me, Mila." And he moves his screen down his body, and I chuckle, as does Mila.

"Wait up. I think you should kiss her pussy first," Hunter chimes in. "She might see your cock and run away." We're all laughing, and I'm glad to see his humor is still there.

Mila talks with them all, laughing and joking, talking about the weather and how she wants it to snow when she kisses me at midnight. I snuggle into her and hold her tight until my phone is at five percent and she tells them all to answer at midnight.

"Our midnight, not yours," I quickly add before they all call out that they love her, and I disconnect the call.

"Beer?" she asks as she reaches into the bag beside us.

"Yeah, if you're having one, I will." I rarely drink. Only at parties in the past, and that was only enough to get me buzzed. I didn't want to end up like my dad, so I mostly avoid drinking.

I open the bottles, and we both take a mouthful. Mila scrunches up her little pink nose, and I laugh. "Not a fan?"

She shakes her head. "Yeah, I don't think I'm a beer-drinking girl. Maybe if I was drunk, it wouldn't taste so bad."

I don't mind. It's not my preferred thing to drink. If I had my way, I would drink her every day. She's the sweetest thing I've ever tasted.

She nestles into my arms, and we look up at the sky, gray and dark. It's not cheerful, but the sounds of the people on the streets below drift up, and I can hear classical music being played. Not something I'm into, but it gives me an idea.

I shuffle backward, and Mila turns to find me standing up.

"You okay?" she asks as she places her beer bottle beside the blanket.

I offer my hand to her, and she takes it. I lift her up, and her eyes widen as she falls into my arms. She places her hand on my chest to steady herself, and I move my other hand to hold her waist.

"What's going on, Roman?" She gives me the cutest look and I kiss her.

I tilt her hand that I'm still holding up into a dance-type pose and start rocking her, side to side to the music playing. Catching on, she rests her head on my chest as I slowly spin us to the music.

After a few minutes of us swaying, she looks up at me with those big blues. "Thank you," she whispers.

I pause. "For what? I'm not a good dancer."

She shakes her head and gives me a small smile. "It's not about how good you are. It's that you do it. For me. For giving me the guys tonight. For just being with me here. In this moment."

"I wouldn't want to be anywhere else in the world," I tell her honestly. I kiss her, softly, not wanting to ruin the moment by it turning into something more than what it is. Tonight is about Mila.

She looks up, and a snowflake falls on her eyelash. She beams and reaches her hand up toward the sky.

I look up too and can see the snow now. Little wet flakes drop on my face, and I look down to Mila. "It's snowing."

She giggles, holding her tongue out to catch flakes. I do the same, and we laugh together. We break apart, holding each other's hands, and dance around the small courtyard and laugh as we catch snowflakes with our tongues. We stop to kiss each other and do it all over again.

I didn't realize I need this as much as she does. This is the first time I have laughed like this in a long time. I feel young and free.

It doesn't take long for the countdown to begin, and the two of us stop dancing. Our eyes find each other, the laughter and games gone. And we count together.

"Three... two... one."

I cup her face in my hands, and she holds my hands there as I kiss her. The sky lights up, and I pull away to see fireworks.

"Happy New Year, Mila."

"Happy New Year, Roman."

My phone is at three percent, so she sends off messages. I apologize for not charging it, but she shakes her head and kisses me.

"Next year, you will have to share me with the three of them. So, this year can be special. Just you and me."

"Let's go inside. I'm frozen, and your nose looks like it's gonna fall off." I bop it with my finger, and she giggles before skipping toward the stairs.

I bend down to get the blanket, and she waves me off.

"Let's get it tomorrow. Right now, I know what I want to start the year off, and it involves your tongue and something else."

I quirk my brow at her, smiling at how playful and light she is right now.

She spins on the spot, her arms out wide, catching snowflakes. I put my icy hands into the pockets of the jacket, and I feel some scrunched up paper in there. I pull it out while she's not looking and glance down to see it has an address on there. Here in New York.

This jacket belongs to Junior, who's missing. I wonder if he's at this address. He is involved, somehow. I just don't know how yet, just that he was here the night of Malcolm's murder and now he's missing, but no one seems that worried. Only his mom. Before Mila notices, I put the paper in my jeans.

She chuckles and snowflakes land on her cheeks. She looks up at me with those big blue eyes, and I know then as I knew before.

I will kill for this girl.

CHAPTER 7
HUNTER

"When's Mom coming home? Can I visit her?" I ask Dad, who finally came home last night. I hadn't seen him in weeks. I don't think I've seen him since before Mila left. Christmas came and went, and he didn't even call.

"I'm not sure. She's very sick."

"What do you mean, she's sick? Is she not in rehab?"

His brows furrow as he looks up from his phone. He can't even talk to me without working. That's all he does... work. Never has time for me. Mom always did. At least, she tried.

"She's in rehab. But addiction is a sickness. Go get ready for school." He waves his hand at me when his phone rings.

I stand there as he answers, greeting the person on the other end with a cheerful hello. When I don't move, he glares at me and waves me off again, dismissing me. I storm out of the room.

Fucking asshole.

Roman has been gone for a week. Mila's still stuck in New York, and I have school. I don't want to go; everyone there knows about Mila and what happened. I hate the way they talk about her in the halls. When they see me, they look at me and whisper. I've skipped a few days, and that's why my dad is here. To make sure I go.

"Can't have a poor attendance record on your report," he told me last night when he turned up here in a brand-new car.

I told him I didn't care about school. I wasn't going to college. He didn't take that well and threatened to kick Roman out of the house. He's not even here. Dad didn't even notice that I'm here. *Alone.*

After grabbing my school stuff, I go out to my car. I hate my car... He got it for me. A gift for my birthday. The only gift he's ever given me. I see his sleek new BMW parked beside mine. I look back to the house then to his new car. I don't give a shit if he sees me on the security camera. Hell, I hope he watches it and see's what I'm about to do. Taking out my house key, since it's the sharpest one I have, I drag it down the driver's side door.

I stand back and assess my work, letting out a small chuckle at the jagged silver line in the black paint.

"Fuck you, Dad." I turn to the house and give him both middle fingers. I hope he loses his shit when he sees his precious car. He doesn't care about me, but he sure as hell will give a shit about that new car.

He can't have anything tarnishing his perfect image. Has to be the perfect boss and perfect father with the perfect son. The perfect wife.

But he's living in denial if he thinks that will ever come true. He fucked us up by never being here. I don't even know the man I share DNA with. My mom drank, and he was never here to notice or care. He was too busy off having affairs and not giving a shit if she knew about them. Never hiding them and threatening her with taking everything if she left him.

No, the perfect man can't get divorced. It would look bad on him. A failure. He can't ever fail. I clench my fists and stare at the house. I loved this house growing up. All the memories I had with my friends. My mom. But now it's an empty shell. The only thing it holds is my father, and I want to burn it down.

I take off to school… *Lakeview*. I fucking hate it there. All my friends are at Ridgecrest. Jace, the boys on the football team. Emerson… Hell, I haven't seen him in weeks. Mila's friends Cadence and Sadie. I miss them all. The only people who give a shit about me at Lakeview are Walker and Asher. And even Asher's been avoiding me.

Hell, I would too after I let all my pent-up anger and rage spill onto his damn face. I feel so guilty, but then the guilt turns to anger, and I'm back in the same place I started.

I feel heat rising in me, my pulse speeds up, and I have to force myself to look away from the house in the rearview mirror and not turn around and set that baby alight.

"Hey, Hunter. How's mafia girl?" Walker swings his arm over my shoulder and follows me down the hall.

I smile and shake my head at Walker's new nick-name for Mila. She's going to love that name when she's back home. "Still stuck, but Roman's trying to work on something. He has this address he's staking out, looking for her stepbrother."

"My mom loves her. Keeps asking when she will be back. I think she's hoping Mila will punch me." He winks then bursts into laughter.

"What's funny?" I don't get it.

"Oh shit, yeah, you weren't there." He smiles and shakes his head, and I realize it must be some inside joke between them.

He sobers up at my expression. "If she needs money for another lawyer or bail money, just let me know. We want to help."

I nod my thanks. "I'll ask her. James mentioned her lawyer isn't very good, and he wishes he could afford someone with more experience and connections there."

Walker doesn't say anything as we walk down the hall. Everyone is looking at me. I've heard it all before. I'm the boyfriend of a killer. I stare them down until they look away.

I don't know what class Walker has, but it's not with me. He doesn't have any classes with me, but Asher does, and it's the one I'm headed to now.

I stop outside my classroom door, and Walker grabs my arm before I head inside. Turning, I see him tapping his chin with his index finger.

"I'm thinking..." he starts and pauses. His finger points at me to wait.

"Don't hurt yourself," I quip back, and he doesn't laugh.

"Nah, this will actually be good. Hell, why didn't I think of this before?" Walker's eyes are wild, and I don't know what he's doing as he leans in closer to me. "Alessandro," is all he says, and he nods with a grin forming on his face.

I shake my head, not understanding. Maybe Walker's brains are short-circuiting. Maybe that's why Mila needs to punch him. To knock some sense into him.

"I don't get it."

"Mafia girl... she needs connections. He's a mobster."

Is he really suggesting I go to Alessandro and ask him a favor?

"No." I cross my arms over my chest.

"He likes her. He would help."

I groan at the reminder. I swear that guy was trying to make a move on my girl at Roman's party. If Walker noticed, then he probably was.

"Okay, so what? I go and ask him?"

He grins and nods. "Yeah, man. I would come with, but I have a thing."

I quirk my brow. He has a thing? I haven't even told him when I was possibly going to see this mobster.

"Getting my hair done." He gestures to his brown mop that's all styled up. I bet he spends a lot of time making it look like that each day. Messy but styled.

I run my hand over my head. "Maybe you should get my style. Easy maintenance."

Walker rubs his hand over my head and laughs. "My hair is my thing... If I get rid of it, I don't know how good my face will look. We can't all be naturally handsome without hair like some." He winks and starts backing up. "Go to him. Ask him. No harm in trying."

That's not true. There's plenty potential harm from asking a mobster for help. I have no idea what he would want in return, but there's nothing I can offer him.

As I walk into class, I search out Asher. He's wearing the school uniform, but the shirt is all rumpled and his hair isn't in its usual style. To be honest, he looks like shit. I didn't make him look like that. I haven't hit him recently; I've been good. I have no idea why I keep taking out my anger on the guy, but fuck. He's not doing well.

I take a seat next to him, and he flinches away. Does he think I'm going to hit him? I already feel guilty about messing up his face. But you can't tell now, apart from a scar along his hairline.

"I'm sorry," I mutter, because I don't want us to fight. I want us to be good. I don't hate him. I really don't. I just… hell, I think I need to jack off more. Because when I'm around him, sometimes my cock gets confused or some shit… like now.

Like I'm some thirteen-year-old and I got my first boner for no reason. Okay, that didn't happen at thirteen, but it's basically the same thing. Only, it's when Asher's around, and I'm starting to take it out on the guy or some shit. Sexual frustration is what it is. I'm not into guys, but I am into watching. Like when Roman fucks Mila. God, that's hot to watch. And thinking about that isn't helping what's happening in my pants.

Mila's coming back and she's going to be mad as hell when she finds out we have all been fighting.

Okay, that and I've been fighting Asher. She's not going to be happy with me.

"It's okay," he replies after a beat.

I rest my head in my hands and draw in a big breath. "No, it's not okay. I don't know why I keep taking shit out on you. It's not your fault, and I know that. I'm sorry."

I need us to work together. Need someone to come with me to Alessandro. Because I can't go alone. Jace would come with me, but Asher was there that day with Mila. He spoke to Alessandro more than I did. I was the rescue party, for someone who didn't need rescuing. She's the one who did the rescuing.

"Thanks," he mutters.

The teacher starts to drone on about something, and I don't give a shit. I tune her out.

"I need you to come with me after school. There might be a way to help Mila."

He nods, and I settle into my chair, my mind anywhere but here.

"I can't believe I'm doing this again," Asher mumbles from beside me.

I clap his shoulder and squeeze gently, trying to help him calm down. Turns out, he isn't as on board with this idea as I am. And that's saying something, because I'm not into this idea. But what else do we have?

As I stop outside the gates of Alessandro's community, I notice a little dark-haired girl running on the perfectly manicured lawn of one of the first houses in here. A man in a dark suit stands nearby, watching us. His hand moves to his jacket, and my heart races. I'm starting to realize that everyone in this community is part of the mob, including that little girl and her bodyguard.

"I'm here for Alessandro Amato," I tell the guard stationed at the gate. "Names are Hunter and Asher."

The guy eyes me, and I see his gun as he turns to pick up a phone and call the Amato house. I fucking hate this place; it scares me that I'm coming here to ask for a favor. But Walker's right. If anyone can help, it's Alessandro. He'll have the connections or at least be able to point us in the right direction.

Asher's rubbing his hands together in the passenger seat as the gates open. I reach over and stop him. As I hold his hands beneath mine, a strange feeling washes over me. My cock stirs and I hold my breath. *What the fuck?* I roll past the guard before glancing over at Asher, who looks a little pale.

I'm still holding his hands. He hasn't shaken me

off yet. Why not? Is he feeling this thing too? I shake my head. No, I'm just worked up, wired off half a dozen coffees. I need to jack off more. Three times a day should be enough.

"We need to show strength, okay? We can't be showing any weakness."

He looks to my hand and nods. "Yeah. Sorry, strength."

After releasing his hands, I stretch out my hand, and he runs his through his hair and lets out a deep breath. I do the same as I roll up to the big house. Fuck, it's huge. I gotta hype myself up for this shit. Like it's game time. We're on and we're here to win.

"We're good." Asher's dark eyes find mine, and I see the same look I gave Walker reflected in them. "He likes Mila."

I laugh. "Yeah, I know. I hate it, but this might be the thing that brings her home."

"Yeah, you're right. Alessandro doesn't give her butterflies, so I don't think we'll have to see him much after she comes back."

I smile at that. The only type of butterflies she gets with him are the ones that warn you away. She told me herself. I don't think she will be adding more boyfriends. I won't let her. Four is more than enough for one girl, and I'm a cuddle hog.

I wonder if Asher likes to cuddle, then I quickly dismiss that thought as fast as it came to mind. I have to get my head in the game.

I haven't been in Alessandro's house before. Last time, I was on the outside, so walking up to his door and being greeted by a guy in a suit wasn't what I'd been expecting. Asher doesn't question it, so I assume that happened the last time he was here.

"Boys, visiting me so soon? Want to go another round of laser tag?" Alessandro rounds the suit and puts his hand out, and I shake it. Asher does the same. I don't know why I'm so scared of this guy. He's normal. Hell, he's still in his academy shirt and tie from school.

"Nah, can't have you back. You kicked our asses in there," I lightly tease, and he gives me a wicked grin. A shiver runs through my body, reminding me that he's a dangerous man. I have to remember that. He's our age, but I have a feeling he's seen more death this year than we will ever see in our lifetimes. And we're only a week in.

"You come alone?" he asks, looking behind us.

"Yeah, Jace isn't here, and Roman's in New York with Mila."

He gestures us to come sit down. "What are they doing there? A holiday? Romantic getaway?" he asks, and I suddenly realize he has no idea what happened.

Yeah, it was on the news here for a moment. People at Ridgecrest High and Lakeview Prep seem to all know. But outside of our bubble, the story would have just been replaced by another murder or shooting on the news the following night.

Asher leans forward. "You don't know?"

Alessandro gets twitchy, and I'm not sure Asher should have said that.

"She's in trouble," I say. "Her stepfather was murdered, and we think her mom and maybe her stepbrother set it up. She says her mom gave her pills for a headache, which knocked her out. She woke up to Malcolm's dead body in the bed beside her."

Alessandro stands, and I watch his jaw tick a few times. He's processing the information, and I don't know if I should stand or keep sitting. Sitting, I think, is the safe bet.

"How long ago?" he asks.

"Shit… has it been four weeks?" I ask Asher.

"Almost a month," he replies.

"The fuck? You didn't come to me back then?" Alessandro seems upset.

But fuck, how do you tell the guy that you never thought of telling him and are half shitting yourself just from being here. I don't know what he did to Johnny and Carlos, and I never want to. So that's why I've been avoiding him. But instead, I say, "Just, so much happened, and we thought she would be back by now. They did find drugs in Malcolm's system. She said he took the same pills her mother gave her."

He paces a few times, deep in thought. Shit,

maybe Walker was right in coming here. I think Alessandro is the perfect person to come to about a crime. How did I not think of this?

He points at me, and my heart jumps into my throat.

"Why hasn't the stepbrother or mother been arrested?"

"Because Mila was the one found with the knife and covered in his blood. And the stepbrother is missing. Roman has an address he thinks he's at, but he hasn't come up with anything so far. He can only be there to watch the apartment during the day."

"Why the day?"

"He's secretly living in the apartment with Mila and her mom. Mila's mom won't let her have anyone there. No visitors, and her phone's been wired. The maid is keeping him a secret in there."

"Roman's phone clean?"

I shrug. I honestly don't know.

He paces a little more, and I hope he's coming up with some amazing plan, because we need one. "Do you know the address?"

I nod. "I was looking on Google Maps and trying to find out who owns the building, since they might know who rented the apartment. But I'm not that good. I can get the first drop of limited-edition Jordans, but I can't hack into anything to save my life." I bring up the address on my phone and show him.

He takes it and looks over at me. "We will circle back to the Jordans after. Can Roman get out there tonight? I'll have someone meet him and get him a burner phone."

I nod. I don't care what Roman says. "He'll be there."

Alessandro dials a number then takes a seat. He looks over to Asher. "You want some water or juice while you're waiting?" he asks so causally, like we're in a business meeting.

"No, thanks," Asher says, and I see the vein on Alessandro's head bulge just a little. I don't think he likes the word no.

"Yes, I could go for some water," I say.

He smiles and waves to a guy I didn't even see until now. Fuck, where did he come from? He nods his head and leaves the room.

"Arrow," Alessandro calls out, and he sits forward on the white leather couch. "You still on princess duty?" he asks, then the laugh that comes out of him makes him seem so… normal. "Busting your balls, as always."

"Look, I need you for a job tonight. I'll have someone meet you there. I'm looking for a guy…" Alessandro snaps his fingers when I just stare at him talking to some guy named Arrow.

"Malcolm Bradshaw Junior," Asher supplies.

And Alessandro continues talking to this guy. "I'll send you the address, and you give me a time, and I will have one of my guys meet you there. He needs a burner." There's a pause. "Yeah, well, tell princess I say hello too."

He chuckles and hangs up. Looking back at us, his expression reverts to business. It scares me a little how quick he can change. I feel like I'm getting whiplash with this guy.

"Who's her lawyer?"

I shrug, I don't know his name, just some lawyer who's a dick.

"George Batten," Asher answers. "He's terrible and just wants Mila to confess to the murder. He works for her mom."

My mouth drops open. *Fuck*. He knows so much more than I do. I didn't even know Junior's last name. I should have known these things. I'm glad I dragged Asher here. It's good he's living with James; he must be telling them so much more than he tells us.

A bottle of water appears on the coffee table in front of me, and I take it, trying to avoid looking dumb for not knowing more answers. I take a huge mouthful.

"I'm going to call in The Bull. She will be back here in a week. You should have come to me when this first happened. We wouldn't be sitting there. Mila would have been back."

I nod; it's true. I should have thought of him, but I

can't take the credit for this. "It was Walker's idea. He told me to come to you and ask for help."

"Where is he?"

Fuck. How do I tell him that Walker is avoiding him? "He had a hair appointment and couldn't make it."

Alessandro bursts out laughing. "Fuck, that's a good one." But then he sobers. "Is he with his mom? I know she's not doing well. I sent her flowers last week."

He did? What's wrong with Walker's mom? I look to Asher, and he shakes his head slightly and motions with his eyes to the door. He will tell me after.

I stand when Alessandro does, and he shakes my hand, then Asher's, and we're leaving.

As soon as we're outside the gates and driving back home, we both let out shaky breaths.

Asher sinks into the passenger seat. "That guy is intense."

"Tell me what's wrong with Walker's mom."

"She's got cancer, and she's not doing well. Walker doesn't talk to me about it. But from the last time I saw her, I would say it's bad, like terminal."

"Shit, I didn't know."

My mom's sick, in rehab, and I will get her back one day. But Walker's mom is… Shit, I didn't want to think about that.

I then remembered what Walker said earlier. "Why would she want Mila to punch Walker?"

Asher's eyes widen, and then he bursts out laughing, and I really feel out of the loop. "Trust me, if Walker told you that… you don't want to know."

I want to know more than ever now.

CHAPTER 8
MILA

When I turn up for another interrogation, I stand and wait for Grace away from my mom and George. If I can avoid being near them, I will. There's a man looking at me from across the room. I would say he's early forties, dark hair with graying sides. He looks good, older but attractive. But why is he looking at me? I'm not even seventeen yet, and we are in a police station.

When he approaches me, he puts his hand out for me to shake. "Mila Hart, I'm Joe Bulger. I'm here to represent you."

I look to where my mother's standing with George and note the confusion on her face. When did I get a new lawyer? I had no idea this was happening. Shit, did Dad take out a loan so I could have a better lawyer?

"Is my dad paying you? He can't afford you." I don't want this man helping me if it means my dad's going to be in debt.

Roman left last night to go and find Junior; he said he's on to something and he's so close. Hunter's been helping him with tracking Junior down.

I think it's just a matter of time before they find him, and my mom will be behind bars. Because I know she's the one who killed Malcolm if she was the only other person in the apartment as she keeps telling everyone. And I know I didn't kill him. It had to be her.

I don't want to stay at the apartment anymore, if George is working for her... which, I think he is. If so, she's onto me. She will come for me. I don't think she would bother keeping me alive. She has everything she wants. That's why I only eat the food that Mary gives me. I wouldn't put it past my mother to drug me and stage my own suicide.

"I'm here because a friend of yours hired me," Joe says. "He's worried about you. But I'm here to fix this all up."

My mouth drops open. What friend hired this man? Hunter? Does he have the money? Oh shit— Walker. He has this kind of money. Fuck, I can't let him pay this guy; I bet he charges a thousand per hour. His suit is designer and custom. If this guy's good, I'll tell him to stay, and I'll pay Walker back when I get home. Somehow.

Grace approaches me and smiles. I hope it's a good smile. One that tells me she believes me, and I'm being set free.

"Come into the room, Mila. We won't be very long today." She eyes Joe, and he gestures for me to follow her.

I take a seat, and he takes the one beside me and opens his briefcase. There's a manila folder in there with my name on it. After taking out his laptop, he closes his briefcase, and before I can even say anything, he turns to Grace.

"I've been going over all your files, and I have sent over everything I have gathered on Amber Bradshaw and Malcolm Junior Bradshaw. You will release my client into the custody of her father, and she will return home. All future communication will be through me."

My mouth drops open yet again. Can he do that? Am I really going home with my dad? Home to the boys? I don't want to get my hopes up; all my emotions are rolling around deep in my belly.

"I will speak to my boss." Grace nods and leaves the interview room.

"Do you really think I'll be able to go home?"

Joe looks at me, his dark gray eyes really seeing me. "You're a victim, Mila, and I'm here to make sure you go home."

A lump forms in my throat. That's the first time someone has called me a victim. I've known the whole time that I'm not the killer. I haven't even been able to grieve for Malcolm. But he's a victim, just like me, and he didn't deserve to die.

Grace returns with Officer Holliday, and I roll my eyes. I'm not getting out of here. He made up his mind from the start, and he's never going to change it.

But he surprises me. He does a double take at the sight of Joe and freezes. I watch as he visibly swallows and shakes his head a little. I'm confused at his reaction to my new lawyer; does he know him? It only takes a moment before Holliday straightens and takes a seat in the room.

"Joe." He nods to my lawyer, his voice different from how he's been speaking to George. Joe must be a very respected lawyer, and they obviously know each other.

"I presume you've received my files on the case. I don't want to be doing your job, Holliday, but someone has to."

My mouth drops open, and I could catch flies with how long I'm staring at Joe like that. *Holy crap*, Joe has balls. He doesn't even let Holliday answer.

"As you can see, there's no motive for my client to have killed her stepfather. She gains nothing. She's never gained anything from that woman who calls herself her mother. She's a victim in all of this, and she's going to be released into the custody of her father. And he will be granted full custody."

He stops talking, but no one says a word.

So, Joe continues. "You can ask your final questions now while I'm present. All future questions will come through me. You may start."

Joe waves his hand at Holliday, and I'm stunned to silence. I think Holliday is too. He's looking everywhere but at Joe, like he doesn't want to be in the same room as him.

I look back and forth between the two men, and that's when I see it. Holliday has been coming in here and verbally attacking me, making himself look bigger than he really is by being a bully.

Joe comes in here and tells him how it is. He has that big dick energy, and there's only one other person I know who has that kind of power to shut someone up so decisively.

I don't need to ask who sent Joe to me. I've figured that out on my own.

Fuck, this guy works for the mob.

"Are you aware that Malcolm had had a vasectomy? Meaning, he didn't want to have any more children."

I shake my head at Grace. It would be a little weird if Malcolm had told me he'd had a vasectomy. But I know my mom really wanted to have a kid with him, so I'm assuming she knew. She would have had to know… right? They were trying.

"No." It was kind of gross talking about my step-father's balls.

"Do you believe Malcolm asked you to return home to tell you that he was divorcing your mother?"

"Yes."

These are all questions I'd asked them for the past month, but with Joe here, they were finally taking me seriously.

"Do you believe your mother had an affair which resulted in a pregnancy?"

"I don't know."

"We have some test results here that show the baby is not Malcolm's."

My fingers rise to my parted lips. I can't believe she had an affair. No, I can. She did it to my dad. But Malcolm was everything she wanted; he had the money and the connections. She could buy anything she wanted, travel anywhere in the world. I wonder if she knew he'd had a vasectomy?

"Do you know who the father is?" I ask.

They probably don't. I wonder if it's someone with money. I bet it is. But if so, why didn't she just get divorced and marry this other person? Unless he's already married. I don't know if any of the couples we used to see at events were ever really happy. Pretty sure all of them were having affairs.

The officers shuffle some papers around, and Joe points to several. He must have found all this. What have the cops been doing? And how long has he been working to get me out of here?

"Yes, and we now understand what really happened that night you came home."

I hate how they keep calling it *home*. New York has never been my home; that apartment has been nothing but a prison. But I'm glad that, after today, I'll finally be going back home. My real home.

"Can I ask who it is? The father. If you know."

Grace clears her throat and places the paperwork on the table. It makes me nervous when the whole room grows serious. Who could the father be? They would need his DNA to match against. Is it a criminal? The president? The way they are acting is kind of scaring me.

"Malcolm Bradshaw... *Junior*."

What. The. Fuck!

CHAPTER 9
ASHER

unter, Jace, and I sit in the living room, uncomfortable, as Mom hands out snacks. James came back a week ago and asked us all to meet him here to have a "little chat." But I already know about the birds and the bees. The last thing I want is my future stepfather telling me about sex.

"Mila's on the way home, as you all know," he starts, and we nod as Mom leaves the room. She's smiling and winks just before closing the door behind her. *Bah…* this is a sex talk.

"She's only a few hours away." Hunter holds up his phone.

James nods, then looks between me and Hunter.

It's been easy to keep the fights we've had off Mom's radar. But at school… not so much. Hunter and I have been good, and then we have been bad. Seeing Alessandro worked out great for everyone; it was a weird car ride, but I chalked that up to going to see the son of a mafia boss. But we were in the school gym earlier today and, well, it ended in a scuffle, and James was the one to come break us up. Again.

I don't know why—he just attacked me. I'd been doing squats, and he just launched at me, wrestling with me on the mat. He got a few hits in low, and I did the same. But the way he watched me... it gave me shivers. He wasn't mad at me. His eyes were wild but not with anger. With something else.

"Now, I get that you are all in love with my daughter. But she's my daughter and I will always love her. And if that mean she wants all of you, and you love her and will treat her good, then I'm okay with that."

He lets out a deep breath and shakes his head. "Okay, to be honest, I don't get this at all. It's a very unconventional relationship. But the fighting stops now."

He points between Hunter and me. I nod earnestly; I don't want to fight. I like Hunter. I respect him. But there's just something there that gets under my skin, and I think it's the same for him. We're too similar and we clash.

But I will make it work, for Mila.

I'll make anything work for her.

"Hunter, I understand that you're going to join the team," James says. "The Kings could really use a player like you."

And we're back to football talk, which is a much safer topic to be having with James. I was a little concerned he would go into the birds and the bees. And I was not prepared to talk about having sex with his daughter.

"Is this why you're fighting? Because you both play wide receiver?"

I look at Hunter, and his eyes widen a little as they bore into mine. I get what he's trying to say to me—that he doesn't want James to know we've been fighting because of Mila. But are we fighting because of her? Or something else?

I quickly speak up. "Yes, I'm worried he's going to steal my position."

I get a slight nod from Hunter, who adds to the lie. "I love being wide receiver, and I know Asher's going to be your best player next year once Walker goes off to college. I want to play for the Kings, James, but he has my position."

James nods and rubs the scruff on his chin. "Mmm... I can see how this could cause tension between you. Even as friends. Have you ever thought of playing quarterback, Hunter?"

"No, Jace had always been quarterback, and I was never going to compete with my best friend. I enjoy being a wide receiver, but I could always try out for quarterback. Don't think I'll be as good as Walker—" Jace waves his hand and motions to himself. "—or Jace. But maybe if you work with me this summer, I'll be ready to go for tryouts."

"We can practice together," I say. "We'll be on the same team, and it would be good for us. We already have chemistry off the field. It would be good to have it on the field as well."

And then I freeze at what I said. "I didn't mean chemistry, like as in... I meant... ahh." Fuck, what did I mean?

The whole room grows quiet, and I swear I can hear my heart so loud that I panic everyone else can too. Everyone's watching me and wondering what I meant by *chemistry*.

What did I mean? I like Hunter... when he's not being an asshole. Well, to be fair, I've been a dick to him in the past. Look what happened when he spent the night with Mila at Walker's place. He didn't hit me back then, and I deserved it. I've been an asshole too.

He's accepted me into this friend group. I look down at the scar on my hand. Fucker took so long to heal; I swear Roman did that on purpose. I've been on medication to clear that infection.

Despite the history they share together, they let me in. Accepted me as I am... *who I am*.

James clears his throat. "Whatever your relationship is off the field, I don't care. As long as y'all are using protection and are being safe, then I don't want to know about it. But leave it in the locker room. We don't need distractions out there or I won't be putting you on my team."

My mouth drops open. Did he just tell me it's okay to be with Hunter and Mila… if we use protection?

Jace looks over at me, his brow furrowed. Hunter's not looking at me, but he's not speaking either. He's not denying anything, and I don't know what to say. I think this whole thing got more awkward than if James had just given us a full sex talk.

I worry my hands together and look out the window, praying that Mila and Roman will be here any moment to save me from this room.

When I feel a set of hands on mine, I look down, where a caramel-colored hand is holding my hands steady. I look up into Hunter's dark eyes, and he smiles. "It's okay, Asher. I get it—the chemistry."

Holy shit. Is Hunter saying he's into me? No, he's just being nice and trying to help me with this weird, awkward cloud hanging over my head.

James looks over at us and clears his throat. "Okay, this conversation is over. You can all wait here until she gets back. If you want to talk about football or how to cook a steak, you can come to me. If you have relationship issues, that's not me." He stands and gives us all a silent nod before leaving the room.

Jace is the first to speak. "Wow, never in a million years would I have thought James would talk to us about that. Like, yeah, I always thought I would marry Mila one day, so I assumed there would be a *talk*. But that was painful. And it wasn't even directed at me."

Hunter turns to him. "You know you're part of this. Mila's in love with you. She admitted that she wishes she'd kissed you and stopped messing with you. So, get over yourself if you think he wasn't talking to you."

I agree. "He was talking to you."

Jace just eyes where Hunter's hands still hold mine. I feel my cheeks burning as I move my hands and Hunter lets go. "Sorry," he mumbles.

I don't know what's going on. I didn't mean what I said. At least, I didn't until he held my hands, and it's just making me overthink things. Right? He loves Mila. I love her. He wants to be with her for the rest of his life. So do I.

Hell, he has threesomes with Roman, and that guy doesn't like touching. I've picked that up after being around them long enough. He likes it from Mila, but I wouldn't touch him unless he permitted it. Like a hug... I don't want to touch his dick.

But is Hunter into that stuff? Would he like to watch me with Mila... touch me? My cock stirs at the thought. I shuffle to angle myself away from Hunter. I've never had that reaction to another guy before, and I'm confused.

It's probably why we keep fighting. I fought him twice last week, and the feeling was there then.

He quirks a brow at me and glances to my now semi-hard cock. I shake my head. Please don't ask me. Please. I beg him with my eyes. Jace can't see me from this position, but I don't want him to know. Hunter winks at me and stands, throwing a pillow my way and it lands in my lap. I let out a deep breath as I hold it to myself.

"Okay, Jace," Hunter says. "We have around two hours before she's here. How do you want to play this out? You want to kiss her first or wait for her to come to you?"

The guy shakes his head and gestures with his hand at us. "You guys kiss her first. You're her boyfriends, and you haven't seen her in a month. I'll stand back and wait. When she's ready, she'll come to me. Our kiss will be epic."

I'm imagining that dirty dancing scene where Baby runs at Johnny, and I smile. That would've been an epic first kiss. Why didn't I think of something like that when I kissed her for the first time?

"What are you grinning about over there?" Jace throws a pillow at my head, and it hits me just as I turn. He cracks up laughing, and I scowl at him.

"Not gonna tell you now."

"Let's put on a movie and get some rest." Hunter moves to turn out the light. "Because I know I will want to spend as long as I can awake with her tonight. I'm glad James and Kate are letting us crash here."

He gets cozy on the other end of the three-seater, leaving plenty of space between the two of us. And I already feel like that space is a huge hole that I'm going to fall into. I don't want him over there; I want him next to me.

Damn. I need to get my emotions in check, because I'm losing it. I turn on the TV, and the light of it puts the room in a low mood light. It's dark enough that I don't have to worry that Jace can see I got hard. But if he's looking at my dick, he probably wouldn't admit it.

I put on Netflix before throwing the remote to Jace. He can pick the movie. I don't care what he puts on. I'm not going to watch it at all.

Then I remember Mom's warning about allowing the other guys to stay over. "No sex at all. Don't forget the rules," I remind them. Mostly Hunter.

It's the only rule we have under this roof. Which is fine. Hunter has a huge, empty house. We will go there tomorrow if we want to go further than a few cuddles. But that's all I want to do—hold her.

"Sex?" Hunter asks. "I wouldn't dream of it. There's no rule against running my finger down her wet slit as her greedy pussy sucks my two fingers deep into her. Brushing my thumb over her clit as she moans my name…"

And I have a full erection, great. I throw a pillow at Hunter at the same time Jace does, and I hear him moan out, "Hunter, your cock is so big."

I shake my head and chuckle. The guy is ridiculous.

"Fuck you, man," Jace groans. "Now I'm all hard and she's two hours away."

I'm relieved to find I'm not the only one affected. As Hunter palms the front of his jeans, I can see he's hard too. He looks over at me, and our eyes meet. He doesn't change his expression or look away, only rubs his cock over his denim.

I let out a small hiss as the room grows dark at the start of the movie. Then the trumpets start as the bunny appears on the screen, and I sink lower into the couch. Hunter doesn't look away, still palming his cock, and I lick my lips, wetting them. I reach for my own, and it's almost a relief to be able to touch it.

But my sweatpants are in the way. I want to take them down and pull my cock out. Stroke it and have him watch.

"Hey, would your mom mind if I go raid her fridge?" Jace asks. "I skipped dinner and I'm starving."

I'm jolted from my sexual daze, and I sit up straighter, bringing another pillow to my lap before quickly replying, "No, it's fine. I hope you like cake."

Once he leaves the room, closing the door behind him, Hunter turns to me, and I try to ignore him. Pretend to be engrossed in the movie. Is this an English movie? Indian? I have no idea what Jace chose, but I'm really into it all of a sudden.

I feel the couch move a little as Hunter shifts, but I don't look at him as I steady my breathing.

"Asher," he whispers into the dark room. The speakers around us almost drown out his words as there is an elephant stampede and earthquake in the movie, and the little girl hides.

"Hey." He grabs my arm, and I flinch back from his touch.

It felt electric this time, and I don't know what it means. The look on his face tells me that my reaction upset him. He only touched my arm to get my attention. Yet, why did it feel so... *right*? The air in here is so thick, and I swallow down the lump in my throat. When he goes to move away, I reach out and grab his arm. But I overshoot and grab his tee, and he freezes.

I swallow down the lump in my throat. "I love Mila."

"I do too. But..." He leans in closer, and so do I, to hear what he's going to say.

He just watches me, like he's under a spell. And I do the same. But the door to the kitchen opens and light spills in. We break apart like we were doing something... *wrong*. Mila's not here yet. Are these feelings I've been having wrong? Because it's not just today that I've felt them.

They've been there a while. I've just been good at ignoring them.

"Man, your mom makes good cake."

I blink, and the spell is broken.

CHAPTER 10
MILA

As soon as I see the guys, I burst into tears. I don't think I've ever cried as much as I do right now. It's like seeing the house, seeing them, cements in me that this is real. That I'm home.

Hunter is the first to get to me. As he lifts me out of the car, his arms tighten around me and he spins me in the air. "Lala, you're back."

And I realize, in that moment, how scared he must have been. "I'm back, and I'm never leaving again." I kiss him and he keeps spinning me around. We're kissing and half laughing, as if this is all a dream.

Then he starts to cry. I try and wipe the tears, but at the same time, mine fall. I cry that I made him cry, and it becomes a vicious cycle until Asher grabs for me.

"Mila, welcome home," he says and holds me to

his chest as I wrap my arms around him, not wanting to ever let go.

I look up, and he cups my cheek and kisses me. When he smiles, I can see the darkness hasn't left his eyes. So, I reach out and trace my fingers along his jaw, to his lips, and he smiles then bites the tip of my finger. I laugh.

But it's Jace on the sidelines, watching, that causes all the floodgates to open at once. I'd been mad at him, and for no good reason in the end. Because anything can happen in the blink of an eye, and then all the *what ifs* seep in.

After what happened to me, I've decided to take chances. I'm not going to fight what I have with Jace anymore. Because I'm in love with him. As much as I loved teasing him... I want him to be mine.

Asher slowly peels away from me, and I stand there, breathing deeply as Jace takes a step toward me. I run at him, launching myself as he grabs my hips, and I wrap my legs around his waist and peer down at him.

"Mila." I can see the unshed tears in his eyes, and I wipe away all of mine before I grab his face.

"I love you, Jace Montero. I always have," I whisper as I take his mouth with mine. Kissing him feels like I'm finally complete.

His tongue sweeps my lips, and I open for him. It's like I've awakened the beast inside each of us, it happens so fast... like we've been starving for each other all these years.

And I have been. *Starving.*

He pulls away, licking his lips, and he has a cocky grin that I want to wipe off his face with another kiss.

"God, you taste amazing. Like tears and heaven."

I chuckle. That's not what I expected him to say, but it makes my chest feel light and happy.

"I love you, Mila Hart." And he takes my mouth again, groaning as I run my hands through his hair and grip it tight. The butterflies dance in my belly. Jace spins us as we kiss, and I open my eyes to see Roman, Hunter, and Jace watching us, grins on their faces.

I'm finally home.

My dad, I haven't really seen him in weeks. When he found out I was being released to him, he told me he would come get me. But I didn't want Roman to drive all the way alone. Joe said Roman could drive me back if Dad agreed. And he did.

Dad clears his throat, and Jace drops me to my feet quicker than I thought possible. Maybe he didn't want Dad to catch him kissing me. Well, it's too late for that. But at the sight of my dad, I turn into that young girl who wants the protection and unconditional love of her father.

"Daddy." I run to him, and he wraps his arms around me and holds me tight.

He smells like the same aftershave he's always

worn, the same one his father wore, and I let out a small sob. I thought I had lost him. I'd started to think I wouldn't see him again, and I'm so close to the age he was when he lost his mom and dad. I wouldn't know what to do if I didn't have my dad.

"Baby girl," he coos, and I sob louder into his polo.

Why is he always dressed for football? I don't know, but it's Dad and I love that about him. He never changes. He's always the man I can count on when things get bad.

"I'm sorry," I mumble into his chest, and he holds me tighter.

"You have nothing to be sorry for. I overreacted and freaked out. If anyone has to apologize, it's me."

I shake my head. I get it. I would freak out if I caught my daughter going down on her stepbrother. That would be a shock for all.

"Mila." Kate rubs my back from beside him.

I break apart from him and wrap my arms around her. She hugs me tight, and I'm so grateful that she doesn't hate me for what she saw me doing with her son. Kate's so forgiving and understanding. She's the perfect mom, and Asher and Madison have been so lucky.

"It's okay, sweetheart. Let's get you inside and get you a hot chocolate."

I burst into another set of tears. Only these are different. These are for the mother I wish I'd had my whole life, and the woman who treats me like I've always been hers.

Madison is at her side, and I grab her, holding her with us as we hug each other on the front lawn, only lit by the streetlamps and porch light.

"Come inside," Dad says gruffly. I think he's trying to hold back tears. But he shouldn't have to— there's no harm in crying, in showing emotion.

I turn back and look at the four boys waiting there behind me.

They all stand together, watching me and talking to each other. They smile, Roman ruffles Jace's hair, and Hunter laughs at something Asher says.

I'm so happy to be back with them.

Three days in my own bed, my home.

If feels surreal, like the past month was just a bad dream. I opened all my Christmas gifts. I didn't have any to give, which I'd been upset about, so Kate took me shopping. I may have bought the guys the same T-shirt and told them all to wear their gifts to Hunter's place on Saturday. They have no idea they're about to be matching, and I can't wait to see the looks on their faces.

I haven't been back to school. I'm just not ready yet. Honestly, I don't think I'll ever be ready. I have spoken to Dad, and he told me the ball's in my court.

I thought he would be mad that I didn't want to return, but I think working in a school has made him realize how hard it will be for me to return now. Even if I transferred to Lakeview, it wouldn't stop the whispers.

Everyone knows what happened in New York. I've never been one to run from bullies and gossip, but I don't think I can move on from this so easily. It's too big, and I need a fresh start.

I've been thinking about my future, anyway, and I want to do something with art. Roman's been with me during the day. He hasn't returned to school, and I know he mentioned getting his GED and working for Ronnie. That makes sense. He loves tattoos and they're his passion. Ronnie told him to come back next week and start full time.

I'm proud of Roman.

I'm going to miss him wearing that red jersey, but this is what he needs. It's perfect for him.

He's here all night too, having practically moved into Kate's house, and Dad's not impressed.

"Roman sleeps with Asher," was what he told me that second night back.

I agreed. As much as I love having Roman with me all the time, it's good to get a little bit of space at night. Neither boy is allowed to walk in my room after eight p.m., and the door has to be open at all times.

I agreed to that as well. The last time I had a door

closed with a boy behind it... well, I don't want to think about that.

Madison and I have been doing girls' nights from eight till ten, painting each other's nails, talking about boys, and making some TikToks. My being away for a month didn't change anything between us. I like how easily we fell back into our little routine.

We tried to get Asher and Roman to dance in our TikTok. Asher, now he can move; he's good. Roman, not so much. He's a great football player, but that's as much skill as he has when it comes to moving his body. He can't dance to save his life. But that's okay. I love him anyway.

"Do you think, one day, I'll have four boyfriends like you?" Madison asks, looking up from the pink nail polish she's applying to my toes.

"Do you want that many boyfriends? I honestly think I'm crazy at times. They are all so different from each other, yet also the same."

She glances at my door, where across the hall, Asher and Roman are. "Like, Roman's very protective of you and doesn't want to let you out of his sight?"

I nod. "That's part of it, but I love that too. I don't know what my future holds, but I hope it will always include them."

"Is it weird that Mom and your dad are getting married, and Asher is gonna be your stepbrother?"

With a laugh, I drop back onto my bed, put my hands over my face, and groan as Madison giggles. "It's weird, and that's why I tried so hard not to love him. But then it just became too much, and I'm glad." I sit up and look down at her. "Because if Dad hadn't met your mom, then I wouldn't have met you and Asher."

"I'm glad they did. I love having you as a sister."

My mom is having a baby. My... *sister*.

CHAPTER 11
HUNTER

lay down the last cushion and take a step back to inspect the area in front of the TV, ready for tonight's big sleepover with all of us together. I smile down at the T-shirt I'm wearing. I love it. It tells everyone that I'm Mila's boyfriend.

I haven't given her the gift I had specially made before she went to New York. I've been waiting for the right time to give it to her. Just us, alone. I'm hoping to give it to her tomorrow morning when I can take her outside and walk her to the spot.

It's a locket on a gold necklace that has a photo of the four of us—sorry, Asher—when we were about nine years old. The photo was taken by my mother, who I spoke to on the phone yesterday for the first time in months.

She's doing well, and she can't wait to come

home. I can't wait, either. I'm so glad that rehab has returned the mother I thought I'd lost to alcohol.

I hear Roman come in, and I call, "In here."

He said he'd get some beers for us all. Make a night of it. Really, I think he used it as an excuse to see Pinkie and the boys down at the MC. He needed to turn in his cut. Since quitting school and beginning to full time with Ronnie, Roman agreed to be friends with the MC but not join it.

Hell, Mila wouldn't have been happy if he'd joined, and he knew it. Knew he needed to give that family up because he has another one now. And we don't want to see him ever get hurt again. Mila wouldn't be able to handle that, and Roman had the smart sense to realize that too.

Roman rounds the corner—his hair is in a braid Mila did for him—and when I see his tee my mouth drops open. He stops and stares at me. I start laughing, and he just looks at me like I've lost my mind.

But he cracks a smile. "She got us."

Oh yeah, she did. I put my hands on my knees to breathe, but I can't stop the laughter.

"Hey, we're here," Asher calls out only moments later, and Mila comes running into the room.

Her face drops a little, and I shake my head and point at her and Roman and my tee. "Oh, Roman," she says. "I wanted to beat you here. You came early and ruined my surprise."

He grabs her and hauls her to his chest. "You playing us?" he growls playfully, and she giggles.

All our eyes go to Asher, who is standing there looking at the two of us wearing the same T-shirt as him. The one that says, *Property of Mila Hart.*

"Oh, baby, you're gonna pay for this." I press myself against her back, and she practically purrs between Roman and me.

My cock is already getting hard. Hell, just hearing her voice has my cock twitching. She's dressed so causally today—it's perfect for snuggle time in front of the TV—and she wore her hair down again. I love when it's down; it's grown so long in just a month.

"Please tell me that Jace has the same one." Asher chuckles.

Mila just giggles, and she blushes. Oh, man. I grind my now-erect cock into her ass, and she presses back against me. "Settle down, boy. We haven't even started the movie."

"Let's all sit down and wait for your last boyfriend, shall we?" I pull Mila from Roman and drag her down to my big blanket pile.

She snuggles into my side, and we look up to where Jace should be coming in any minute now.

Asher gets his phone out and sits beside me, his leg brushing mine as Roman moves into Mila's other side. "I'm gonna record this. This is just too funny."

"How did we not think about the fact that we are all property of Mila?" I shake my head. I should have thought of that when I put it on, but I was just too excited to wear it, and I guess it was the same for Roman and Asher. Jace better be wearing his, or we're going to have a very upset Mila.

I hear the front door open, and we all sit up. Mila's practically bouncing beside me, and I can't help but feel just as giddy. She got us good, but this is so much fun.

"Hey," Jace calls, and we all call out in return.

Mila holds her hand over her mouth to hold in the giggles, and Jace rounds the corner and pauses in the doorway. He's wearing a Rebels hoodie. What the fuck? He observes us all, drops the bag of goodies, and stares at the T-shirts we're wearing.

Mila frowns. "You didn't wear it," she says, no longer happy.

I glare at Jace. How could he not wear it? It was the one thing Mila asked us to do.

He pulls up his hoodie to reveal *Property of Mila Hart*, and she claps her hands and giggles.

"It was a little chilly," he tells her with a shrug.

I nod for him to take it off. I know it's cold out today, but she wants us to all be wearing matching shirts, like we're quads or some shit. But I love the way it makes her laugh, something that hasn't come as freely as it did before New York.

Jace brings in his bag and dumps it in front of us. Mila starts raiding it, snatching out all the candies she loves.

She chucks some Reese's cups into my lap and tosses Skittles to Roman. Asher holds out his hands when she pulls out the M&M's, but she holds them to her chest and says, "My precious."

I laugh, grabbing and holding her to me as I whisper, "You're my precious. Can I eat you later?"

She turns her face to me, looking at me with those big blue eyes. "You better." She kisses my lips briefly and reaches for Jace, who kneels near her feet.

She looks at us all and bites her lip.

"What's put that expression on your face?" Asher asks.

"Just how this is supposed to work with four of you."

I shake my head. "Well, I can tell you how it's gonna work... You do have two hands and three holes."

Her brows raise and I smirk. Yeah, I have thought about it, okay?

"I meant, when we're all snuggling and stuff. Do we rotate? Do we have certain nights? I didn't think this part through at all."

She seems worried. I don't know why; it hasn't been a problem before. "We can work that out as we go along. It doesn't need much thought. We will just do what we feel is best, take turns and all that. Don't you worry about it."

I look to Asher, and I don't know why. Probably because the fact that he chose to sit beside me is making me think I need to talk to him about the same things I did with Roman. Maybe, this time, it will be less of a one-sided speech.

"Actually, now we're all here, we need to have the sex talk," I say.

Jace grins. "I consent to it all."

And I raise my brow. Does he have any idea what he just said? "So, you consent to sucking my cock?"

Jace makes a sound in the back of his throat and starts coughing.

"What are you choking on?" I ask him. Did he eat an M&M?

He shakes his head, and Mila grins at me. "Not your cock, that's for sure."

I burst out laughing. Everyone joins in, and poor Jace has tears in his eyes as he tries to clear his throat.

"I was eating when you said that. Give a guy a warning before you hypothetically put your cock in my mouth. And that would be a no, I don't consent to that."

"Okay, so you get what I'm trying to get at here now, Jace?"

He nods. I look to Asher, and he does the same.

"I've had this talk with Roman already, but I think it's best to get it out of the way before anything goes further and we find ourselves in a situation where someone's uncomfortable."

Mila sits up and clears her throat. "So, basically,

are you okay if someone, other than me, touches you in a sexual way?" She looks to Jace.

He shakes his head. Mila turns to Asher, and his eyes dart to me for a split second, and Mila grips my thigh tighter. Oh shit. I hold my breath for his answer.

He looks away as he shakes his head. I deflate a little. I don't know if I'm ready for that myself. Or if it is something I want to do. She saw it, though. There's something between us, even if we're not ready to take that next step.

"We can come back to this conversation in the future, when we're all more comfortable with each other. But this has to be a judgment-free zone. And we need to communicate to make this all work together," I tell them all.

"There might be accidental touching," I say. "We've all confirmed there is to be no sexual touching, except for with Mila. And it's easy to accidentally touch, okay? It doesn't mean anything. It's an accidental cock graze or ball touch."

Jace chuckles, and he will soon find out what I mean by that.

"But I want you to know that I respect all your boundaries. And I consent to be touched... in a sexual way."

Roman turns to me and his eyes widen. I shrug. I want to see what happens, if being touched by another guy turns me on. Or is it just the thought of being touched by a guy that does? Or maybe it's just Asher; something about him gets my blood boiling, and I want to fight him. Or do I want to fuck him? I haven't quite worked that out.

"Okay, lets watch our movie and eat some candy." Mila snuggles in beside me again and Roman moves over so Jace can be on her other side. Mila smiles, and I kiss her nose. "See, we will make it work."

Mila jumps up as soon as the movie ends. We'd watched *The Secret Garden*. Which was not something I had planned on watching, but Jace put it on the other night while we were waiting for her, and I know Mila used to love this movie when she was little. She loved it again now.

"I gotta pee." She dashes off to the restroom, and I sit up and look around at everyone.

"Next movie, can we make it sexier? Because I felt very uncomfortable watching this kids' movie with a hard-on while being pressed against her."

Jace chuckled and nodded. "I agree. That was a little weird, but I wanted this to be a nice night for her. Like old times when we used to do this."

I get where he was coming from, and it makes total sense. She needs a reset after all the shit that happened to her. Old, happy memories are good.

Just, my dick has a mind of its own when Mila is involved.

Mila doesn't take long to return. As she stands and watches the four of us, I'm curious what her next move will be. I wink over at her, and I put my hands out for her to come. I want her on my lap.

She had the same idea, it seems. As she lowers herself onto me, my hands grab her ass as I grind my erection against her. Roman runs his hands through her hair and kisses her.

This is the first time Asher and Jace have been here for this, and I'm not sure how this is all going to work the first time. It might take a little while before things flow and we work out a system. But I know one thing—Mila will be very pleased.

"Mmm…" she moans.

Watching her and Roman devour each other. Rubbing myself against her, drawing those sweet sounds from her. Until they break apart.

"My turn." I kiss her with the passion and intensity of a man who missed his soulmate. She is the love of my life, and I missed her so much. But now that she's back, I want to show her how good I'm going to make her feel tonight.

Asher's the next to move in, taking her face from my hands and kissing her. Her long blonde hair cascades down her back. I gather it up in my hand, and when I feel that Asher's had enough, I pull her away.

She stares down at me, her eyes glazing over with need as she gives me a lazy smile.

"You've had enough Asher. It's Jace's turn."

Mila turns to Jace, who shuffles in closer. He doesn't look as comfortable as the rest of us in this moment, so I nudge her off my lap to go to him. She crawls on all fours, her ass swaying, and I groan at the sight, palming my cock over my sweats. She sits up on her knees and pulls Jace by his tee.

"Isn't she gorgeous, Jace?" I prod. "Kiss her and show her how much you've missed her."

Mila moans into his mouth as he pulls her close to him. The sound of her has my cock twitching in my sweats. I didn't wear boxers; I wanted to make it easier for when I bury my cock deep inside her and make her come over and over.

Roman surprises me by moving up behind her and lifting her tee over her head while Jace holds her, his eyes drifting down to her black bra.

I lick my lips, wanting to taste her. "Are her nipples hard?" I ask Jace, and he swallows as he nods. Jace has always been the one in charge for the past four years. But now, Mila is.

And I'm just happy to help direct. "Touch them, suck them. She needs it. Don't you, babe?"

Mila throws her head back, thrusting her chest at Jace. Yeah, she needs to have her pretty little nipples touched.

My hand goes under my waistband, and I grip

my hard cock. A small moan escapes my mouth as I stroke myself to my girl and my best friend.

Only, Jace is stiff in his motions, and I'm not sure if it's because he's going first and he needs to warm up to the group experience, or if he's really nervous about being with Mila in front of us.

"Mila, babe." She practically moans to me. "Asher needs some attention."

I need her to come here so I can show Jace how this works. That we don't care if we see each other pleasing her. I'm not here to look at his dick. Yeah, I've seen it; it's not a big deal. Once he sees Roman's, he's probably going to cry.

Mila crawls to us, and Roman tugs at her sweatpants, pulling them down before she gets to Asher, who's up on his knees, ready to kiss her and give her nipples the attention they deserve.

Asher takes her mouth with a brutal kiss that has my cock leaking pre-cum. If I keep this up, I'm gonna blow before I even touch her... Actually, that's not a bad thing. I'll probably blow my load the second she sits on my dick, so if I blow now, I will last longer when she touches me.

Roman pushes Mila forward so she's on all fours over Asher, who's now lying beneath her. Roman's so confident now that he doesn't even need me to say anything. He just knows what our girl needs and takes care of it. Hell, he's been taking care of her for weeks alone. He doesn't need help anymore.

He looks over at me, like he knows I'm thinking about him. Asher removes her bra and Roman winks at me. I almost don't know how to react to that.

Roman Valentine winked… at me. I almost laugh, but then his large hand goes to her back, and he presses her against Asher's chest, her ass in the air, and I watch as he moves between her legs and licks her from clit to ass.

"Fuck," Jace mutters from where he's still watching.

And Mila lets out all kinds of words and sounds as Roman licks her again. I squeeze my cock to stop myself from coming now. I want to pace this out a little more.

I motion over to Jace, and his eyes find mine. I mouth, *"Are you okay?"*

He shrugs, then shakes his head.

"You want to just watch?" It's fine if that makes him feel more comfortable. I don't want him weirding out and making Mila upset, so I need him to be on board or to quietly leave. Jace doesn't say anything, he just keeps watching.

I watch as Asher moves his body up from under Mila, until his dick is pressing against his boxers. When did he lose the jeans? Fuck, that was good. I bite my lip and stroke myself, waiting for her to take his cock out and suck it.

Mila moans as Roman fucks her with his fingers, sucking on her clit and driving her wild.

"Pull down his boxers, babe. Show Asher what he's been missing."

Asher gapes at me, his eyes finding mine in the darkened room. Hell, if he's not used to my dirty mouth from all the times he listened to us through the bedroom door, then he's got a lot more surprises coming his way.

Her mouth lowers over his cock, and he moans deeply, his hand going to her hair as she works him with her mouth.

Dang. I was too busy looking into his eyes to see what he's packing.

"Okay, um… I can't do this group thing. I'll be up in your room, Hunter." Jace stands suddenly and before anyone can speak, he's gone.

The audible pop of Mila's mouth has me turning to her. She's looking in the direction he just left, and I can see she's worried.

"It's all good, babe. He just needs time before he shares. He told me that before."

She nods, but glances at the door one more time before she sucks Asher into her mouth.

He groans. "Shit, Mila. I think I'm gonna come."

Mila doesn't let up, and I watch as Asher's abs tighten and his body bucks gently, wanting to push her away yet keep her there at the same time.

He lets out a loud groan. "Fuck, I'm coming," he calls out.

She still doesn't let up, and I watch him come undone.

"Fuck," I hiss, gripping my own cock hard to stop myself from coming. That was so hot.

"That was fast." Mila giggles as she sits up a little and licks the corner of her mouth, tasting him on her lips.

I don't think; I just move in and lick the seam of her lips. She gasps as I take her mouth and taste Asher on her.

"Fuck," Asher whispers beneath her, and I smirk.

Not yet.

CHAPTER 12
MILA

oly shit.

Hunter just kissed Asher off my lips. I'm speechless. I didn't know that was something I'd be into, but I sure as hell unlocked a new kink. *Fuck, yes.* I want more.

When Hunter announced that he was okay with being touched sexually, I'd been surprised. I didn't know he was into that. But I'd been excited at the thought of watching someone touch him... lick his abs. My core clenches at the thought of Asher going down on Hunter's cock and sucking him dry.

I wasn't too sure how all of this would work. Moving from being friends for so long then moving into this new territory with Roman and Hunter has been exciting. But I know Jace is different. He left the room; he didn't want to join in. So, I need to find him when I'm done here. Speak to him and ask him why he left.

Asher's still getting to know everyone. But I think the fact he doesn't have that same history is why he's so comfortable here.

Roman was very clear in the past that he had no desire to touch Hunter. But I don't know if that's going to change now. Of them all, Hunter seems the most open to new experiences. I wonder if he's ever kissed a boy before.

Now that's all I'm thinking about, and I really want him to kiss Asher. But I'm not too sure how Asher feels about that. He was hesitant about the touching thing, but I think, with Hunter, it's different than if it was one of the other guys touching him. I want to get the two of them alone so I can see what will happen.

Roman lifts me and spins me so I'm straddling him. I run my hands over his chest, and he grips my hips as I rub myself against his hard length, spreading my wetness over him. I see the heat in his gaze.

"I need to feel you," he moans.

As I bend over and lick his nipple, his hand goes to my hair, and he holds me there as I tease it with my tongue, nipping and sucking. He bucks up, and I feel the pleasure deep within my core. I need him inside me, badly.

Sitting up, I straddle him as I grip his thick length. I feel Asher and Hunter move closer. I rub the tip of Roman's cock through my wetness and tease him as he groans, gripping my hip tighter. I give him a sly smile. I love to tease him just as much as he teases me.

"You gonna sit on his big, fat cock, baby?"

My body breaks out in a shiver at Hunter's words. *Dirty mouth.* I smirk over at Hunter, and our eyes meet. I don't look away as I slowly lower myself onto Roman's cock. The stretch burns so good. I gasp at the full feeling I get when I fuck him.

Roman's hand comes up and wraps around my throat. I love to give him control; it turns me on so much to surrender while he gives me pleasure.

He keeps one hand on my hip and the other around my throat as I start to ride him. Feeling fingers brush over my nipples and a hand trailing down my belly, I jolt forward when it rubs against my clit. I open my eyes and find Hunter there, his fingers working my nub. Higher and higher. I'm calling out to Roman... Hunter... Asher as he pinches my nipples and the pleasure shoots straight to my core until I'm gasping for air. I come around Roman's cock, my pussy clenching him tight.

"Fuck, fuck..." Roman groans out as his movements become erratic and he spills inside of me. He lets out a deep, shuddering breath as he gazes up at me from the floor, his heart racing under my hands just as fast as mine.

A fine sheen of sweat coats my body, and Asher runs his hands all over me, touching me in places I didn't even know would turn me on.

"You took his cock so good, babe," Hunter praises me.

Roman lets go of my throat, dragging his hand down between my breasts and down to my clit. He rubs against my little nub with his thumb, and my body reacts for the split second before he pulls away. His hands fall back over his head, and he lets out a deep breath.

"Let me feel how wet you are now." Hunter moves his hands lower, to where Roman's still hard inside me.

Roman's brow raises as he watches Hunter's finger rub my clit before moving down just that little bit lower. "I want to feel from the inside," Hunter says.

I don't know how to answer that, and I don't have to. He pushes his finger inside me, and the stretch burns a little with Roman's cock already still nestled deep inside me. It's tight and full. But as Hunter starts working my G-spot, I can feel Roman growing harder beneath me.

This is a gray area, but Roman hasn't spoken up to say he's not comfortable with it. He's watching where his cock and Hunter's finger work me.

I hold Hunter's wrist and start working myself against him. It's such a strange feeling, but at the same time, feels amazing. I moan and play with my breast, rolling my nipple around my fingers. I can feel Asher behind me. I'm not sure what he's going to do, but my skin prickles with anticipation.

He wraps my hair in his fist and pulls so my head tilts back to look at him, and he takes me in an upside-down kiss, nipping and licking until it's too much and I crash down around Hunter's finger and Roman's cock. I pant and shudder as Hunter keeps working his finger, prolonging my orgasm until I push him away.

"That orgasm was something else," I finally get out, trying to catch my breath.

Roman lets out a grunt, and I bend down and kiss him. His cock is hard, but I know a second round will take a while, and I need a few moments.

I get up on shaky legs and stand naked in front of the three of them. The way they all look up at me makes me feel so powerful. Like the most beautiful woman they've ever seen. At least, that's how I feel about them as I watch them all.

Hunter's the only one who hasn't come yet, and I want him to come inside me. He must read my mind since his fingertips trail up the inside of my thigh until he meets me at my core. My legs shake a little. I need him so badly.

I feel Roman's cum leak out of me. It trickles

down the inside of my thigh, and Hunter doesn't miss it with his eyes. He runs the tip of his finger to catch it, and I gasp in surprise when he pushes it back inside me.

He fucks me with his fingers, looking up at me from where he sits on the blankets. I wish he had his curls back; I want to grab his hair and thrust his face to lick it all up. Lick Roman from my pussy. But I can't force him. He said he was open to being touched... not to eating his best friend's cum from my·pussy. If he wants to eat me out, he will.

His thumb finds my oversensitive clit, and I stumble into him. He chuckles and Asher does too. I turn to see Roman watching us from his post-orgasmic bliss, lazily stroking his cock. He doesn't seem fazed that our friend fucked me with his finger and his cock. I'm glad, because I want that to happen again.

Hunter grabs my waist and flips me down on my back, pouncing on me before I can even register what just happened. "My heart," he purrs into my ear, nipping my lobe.

"I love you, Hunter," I whisper as I kiss him.

With a smirk, he lowers himself down my body and kisses my stomach. I watch him, my breaths coming out rapidly, as he kisses his way down.

Hunter spreads my legs and bends my knee over his shoulder. I hold my breath at his next move. He keeps his eyes locked on mine as he lowers himself down and kisses me right where I want him to. My eyes widen as he runs his finger down my wet folds and then licks me from my core to my clit. I gasp at his tongue as he works my body, tasting Roman on me.

I watch Roman. He's now sitting up, watching Hunter. He's no longer touching himself. Hunter is tasting him from me like it's his last meal. I glance back at Asher, and he's watching us, stroking himself to the sight.

My back arches as Hunter fucks me with his fingers, his mouth never letting up the assault on my clit, and I cry out as the pleasure rips though me. He doesn't stop. He moves, taking my mouth as he sinks his cock deep inside me. He presses my knee against my chest, hitting deeper, and I moan. I reach out to Asher; I want to stroke him. My hand grabs for his cock, and when he gets close enough he hisses.

"Mila, god, you're beautiful." Asher strokes my cheek as I stroke his length, matching the pace Hunter sets.

Over and over, our bodies making sounds as we pant and grunt, the pleasure always just there, so close, and I don't think I have it in me to come again. I've come so much tonight, I think I'm all orgasmed out.

Asher grips my hand and uses it to set his own punishing pace. It only takes a few seconds before he's moaning his release. Jets of his warm cum spray onto my chest, and Hunter pauses as he watches it unfold.

Asher's body shakes, and he grunts before falling beside me and kissing my shoulder. "Holy fuck. I think I died and went to heaven tonight." He lets out a deep breath and sinks into the cushions, a lazy smile on his face as he watches me, our faces so close that I could kiss him.

Before I can, Hunter says, "Imagine that every night," as he slams back into me, his thumb rubbing my clit as he looks between us. He pants as he brings me closer and closer to release. I'm grasping his arms and begging him to let me come. I don't want to wait; I want it now.

Hunter kisses me—it's rough and hot. He pulls back and looks at Asher. I turn my head, and Asher's mouth takes mine. I gasp as his tongue sweeps over mine. Hunter doesn't let up, and Asher's fingers stroke my nipples. I gasp and pull away when I feel Hunter's hand on my breast, rubbing Asher's cum into my skin.

Hunter leans down and takes a nipple into his mouth and sucks, nipping, and pulls away. He looks down at Asher, and I turn to see his eyes full of heat. Fuck. Asher liked that. I did too.

Hunter licks his lips, and never letting up, he pounds into me harder now. I hitch my leg higher, and he reaches that sweet spot that has me gasping.

Asher pulls the back of Hunter's neck and presses

his forehead against him. The two of them stare into each other's eyes, and I'm worried to make a sound and stop whatever's happening here. Because, holy shit, this night is just getting started if they're about to kiss.

But Hunter grunts, his cock swelling with release as he comes deep inside me. I want Asher to kiss him; Hunter won't make the first move. I know that he's waiting on Asher to decide what he wants.

I take Hunter's chin and tilt his face to mine. I kiss him gently, then I turn to Asher and lean over, kissing him, then pull away. I look to them both, and they turn to each other.

Asher hesitates for a moment before brushing his lips softly over Hunter's. He pulls away, but Hunter won't let him. That was enough permission for him to chase that kiss. Hunter grips Asher's throat and pulls him in, deepening the kiss as Hunter rocks into me, his cock still hard, and just the sight of them kissing has me coming.

I crash down, unable to move. Hunter slides off me and lies on his back beside me. I look back at Roman and find his eyes closed, and he's lightly snoring. I need to get cleaned up, but I'm exhausted.

I'll just close my eyes for a moment.

I feel someone lifting me into his arms. I sigh into his chest. I don't know who it is; it's not Roman or Hunter. Maybe it's Asher, taking me to bed. I reach up and feel the stubble of hair on his chin. I trace my fingers up to his lips, and I feel a nip, then he kisses my finger. I smile.

It's Jace.

CHAPTER 13
JACE

Jealousy's a bitch.

I don't know why. I just couldn't watch them with her. I'd seen her kissing Roman and Hunter, and I'd been jealous. I wanted that too.

Then Mila kissed me. And I wanted more. I wanted to feel her sweet body naked under mine, wanted to taste her and have her coming around my tongue. Hell, she was my first kiss. Even if I wasn't hers—not going ask her; it's me, I know it—I want another first, but all her firsts have been taken. If not with guys in New York... Hunter has been with her for months, and I'm sure they have gotten up to a lot of things. He seemed very in control tonight. I didn't know he was so dominant.

I got jealous watching her with them all. I didn't know how to act in this group situation, then I felt like a fifth wheel. I didn't want them touching her. I wanted to do all the touching.

She's mine.

So, instead, I did the next best thing. I left the room. I wasn't comfortable. I wanted to punch Asher when she sucked his cock. So, I removed myself from the room and came up here to the guest room. The one with the big bathtub. It's not as big as Hunter's parents' one, but this is plenty big for two.

I thought I would find her after and do a first with her that I never did with a girl. I ran her a bath. I knew she would need to wash off after her sex session. I shake my head, not wanting to think about it. I've decided watching isn't my thing. I hope Mila understands I don't want to partake in any group activities. I don't think I can.

I love her. I just don't want to share her.

"Mila, beautiful?" I smile down at her in my arms.

She gives me a sleepy smile, and her eyes crack open a little as she focuses on me. "Hey, handsome." Her voice is deep from sleep, and I chuckle a little. She's so tired. The guys wore her out. But I'm about to take care of her. She can sleep after she relaxes.

"I ran you a bath. I want to massage you and let you soak for a while."

She moans, and the sound goes straight to my cock. That wasn't the plan. I really only wanted to give her a bath.

I place her on the edge of the bath, and she looks down at the bubbles. She reaches in and swirls her hand around the hot water. "Mmm... a bath sounds amazing." She looks down at herself. She was wrapped in a blanket when I stole her from the puppy pile out there. Opening it a little, she looks down at herself then back up at me. "Are you coming in the bath with me?" She peers up at me with those big eyes.

"Yes, I thought I could massage your shoulders."

She moans at that and rolls her neck. "I'll just have a shower first," she says as she stands.

I stand up straighter. Why does she want to shower? The bath is ready to go. "Is it too hot?" I ask. I thought girls liked hot baths. My mom does; maybe it's just my mom who likes it hot.

Her eyes widen, and she shakes her head. "No, it's perfect. It's just, I have..." She waves down at her body, and my eyes widen. *Oh shit.* She's got the guys on her.

"Oh, yes, a shower first." That's very thoughtful of her. I can't get jealous or grossed out by that. She's thinking of me, after all. I quickly rush over and start the hot water, testing it until I can turn the cold on. She smiles shyly at me as she drops the blanket in front of me, exposing herself, and she is a sight.

I whistle lowly at her, and she giggles, the shyness leaving. She steps into the shower, and I move back to sit on the edge of the huge tub. She smiles over her shoulder at me as she washes her body, tipping her head back and letting the water run over her face and hair.

She's the most beautiful woman in the world. No one compares to Mila Hart.

I readjust my cock in my pants, but it's no use. She wiggles her sexy little ass, and I chuckle. She knows I'm watching her.

"I love your perfect little ass." *She's mine.*

I quickly strip and get into the bath water. Fuck, it's hot, and I swear I just burned my balls. But I'm in and ready for Mila. My balls might take a week to recover from that scalding.

I hear her turn off the shower, and her little feet pad across the tiles to the bath. I crack open an eye to catch her leg swinging over the tub. As soon as both feet are in, I pull her down to sit between my legs. Only, she's surprised at the sudden movement and loses her footing and slips. Her ass crashes to my chest, and I let out a strangled sound as the air leaves my lungs, and then she slips down my chest and crushes my cock. I jerk away at the sudden pain.

"Fuck," I hiss out and she scrambles away.

"Oh shit. I'm so sorry. The bath is slippery, and when you pulled me, I lost all traction. Did I break your dick?" Her brows are mashed together, and she looks at my face, trying to gauge how bad it is from my expression.

It's bad. I don't think my cock is ever going to

work again. Okay, I think it might just be sore for a day or two. I wasn't planning on using it tonight, anyway. So, it's fine.

"Nah, just a little tender, so go easy on the poor guy."

She giggles. Moving closer, she kisses me.

I cup her face and deepen the kiss. God, she tastes amazing, like… I pull away suddenly. Holy shit. She didn't brush her teeth. It's been a few hours, but still… Am I tasting Asher's cum? Am I cool with that? Fuck if I'm not, because I'm going to have to get used to their cum on her and in her. I don't want to make a habit of asking her to brush her teeth every time I want to kiss her.

"Are you okay? Is your dick hurting? Do you want me to have a look?"

I burst out laughing, and she does too. I'm glad she's not upset by my reaction, but I need to tell her. She said this only works with communication, and I'll only learn if I open my mouth.

"No, it's just…" I take a deep breath. I get too into my head, and then I get myself into situations that I make myself and end up alone. I don't want to be the one on the outside again. "I was just thinking about cum."

How do I word this without sounding like a total dick?

"Your cum? Do you think there is permanent damage down there?"

What? I let out a breath and drag my hand down my face. The bubbles stick to my nose, and I blow them off and shake my head.

"No, my dick and cum are just fine. It's the others' cum. Just like, now, when I was kissing you, am I tasting them on there? I don't want to think like that. But now I have it in my head, and this relaxing bath isn't going so well. And I'm trying to talk it out so it doesn't become a thing…"

She puts her hand on my mouth. "It's okay. It's not gonna be easy for everyone at first. We have to find our rhythm, and we will. It just takes time. You're the newest to this. You've seen us kiss and that was okay?"

I nod.

"But tonight, it's all new, the stuff behind closed doors. I don't have to be jealous since I get all of you. But this is why talking out feelings is good. It's the only way this can work, and I want this. I want it to work for us all."

I do too. I pull her in and kiss her. She hesitates, but I sweep my tongue over her lips, and she parts for me. Her tongue meets mine and she slowly melts against me, being careful of my poor cock.

When we finally pull apart for air, she sighs. "I love kissing you. I can't believe I teased you for so long and this is what I was missing out on."

I take her small hand in mine and lower it under the bubbles to my cock, which is hard as a rock and doesn't seem to care that it was almost crushed to death ten minutes ago.

"Mmm... I have been missing out on this too," she says. "But I have already tasted you and I know I like it."

My mouth drops open at the memory of that morning when she worked herself beside me on my bed, and I came from her tasting me. That was one of the most intense orgasms I've ever had.

"But no more of this tonight," I tell her. "He's just always happy to see you. Let me massage you. I bet the guys gave you a workout."

She turns her back to me, nestling between my thighs, being careful not to hurt my dick again. Not that the first time was her fault.

I grip her shoulders and start working out the knots. She groans, and my cock responds as she rubs up against me, and I have to stop her.

"As much as he's happy to see you, he's still a little sore from the ass accident earlier."

She stops and turns her head to look at me over her shoulder. "I'm sorry... should I kiss him better?" She grins wildly at me.

"Maybe tomorrow? He needs a little rest."

She pouts.

I chuckle. "Haven't you had enough dick tonight?"

"I didn't get to taste yours."

Well, fuck.

CHAPTER 14
MILA

I wake snuggled tight in Jace's arms. It's much nicer than sleeping on the pillow fort Hunter made for us last night. As much as I loved them as kids, a bed is always softer on the body.

I'm surprised the others didn't come looking for us, but I guess they're giving us some time alone, which I'm very grateful for. Last night was hot, like crazy-sexy-I-want-Asher-and-Hunter-to-kiss-again-while-I-watch hot.

I stretch, and my body aches in all the best ways. Jace hugs me tighter and I smile.

"Good morning, beautiful." He kisses my forehead.

I groan, not wanting to get up, but my tummy rumbles, and I know I need to eat something soon. "How's your dick?"

His chest rumbles as he chuckles. "I think he's all better now."

I run my hand down his chest and under the sheets and find him hard. I wrap my fingers around his cock and give him a playful squeeze. "I think he's happy to see me."

He cocks a brow at me, and I smirk, stroking him. "Mmm…"

The next thing I know, my hand is being snatched away as he rolls on top of me. I'm on my back, and he's nestled between my legs. We're both naked from the bath, and I can feel his hard cock between my legs.

He kisses my nose, and my tummy rumbles. I groan. Ugh… like, give me a few minutes here, tummy. I will feed you after.

He pulls back and looks down into my eyes. "I can think of many different things I want to do with you right now, but the only thing I'm going to do is feed you." He grinds his erection into me, and I grip his ass cheeks to keep him close, little sparks waking up my body. I can eat after, right? My tummy rumbles again. *Fuck.*

"Your cock?" I tease.

He gives me a wicked grin, and as much as I want to play around, I really do need to pee and eat. And brush my hair; it's a mess after the bath.

"Let's get you up, dressed, and fed. I bet Hunter has something going out there. I swear I saw bacon in the fridge yesterday, so I hope he's cooking that up."

Oh man, bacon, eggs… pancakes? Yes. I scramble out of the bed, my feet getting tangled in the sheet as I look around the room for clothes. I want breakfast.

Jace laughs. "Yeah, you only had a blanket, remember? Where's your bag of clothes?"

I stop looking for clothes and realize I left it in the car. I roll my eyes. "In the car. Can I borrow your shirt?"

Jace gets out of bed and stands there like a Greek god—one with a really nice cock. He sees me looking at him, naked like this. Now that he's mine, I can't help myself. I go to him and run my hand down his chest. Fuck, he feels good.

"I left my shirt out there, Mila."

Huh. Well, it's not like they haven't all seen me naked. I shrug and turn to the door. Jace calls out for me to wait, but I don't as I stroll out to the living room in hunt of clothes.

I pass the kitchen and smell the yummy scents coming from there. Roman's in there, cooking, Hunter is setting the table, and Asher is pouring orange juice into glasses. They all stop and look at me as I walk past, naked.

Hunter wolf whistles at me, and I giggle.

"Fuck, Mila. Come take a seat." Asher waves over, and I shake my head.

"I need to wear something. Just gonna grab my clothes from last night."

Roman calls out, "Mila," and I freeze. I watch as he approaches me, his hand going to the hem of his *Property of Mila Hart* tee and, in one swift move, it's over his head, and his sexy body and tattoos are all on display.

Fuck, I think to myself. *I got so lucky with all of them.* They're all athletic and hot as sin. And man, I wanna lick his abs for breakfast.

Roman's brow rises, and I realize I said that out loud. Hunter is laughing, and I shake my head.

"Well, who can blame me? Roman has abs for days. My big Viking." I love that his hair is still in braids. It's a little fuzzy from sleep, but I will just do them again later when we're watching TV or just sitting around shooting the shit.

I lift my arms and Roman slips the tee over my head. It's warm and smells like him... and bacon. "Mmm, yummy."

He kisses me and slaps my ass. I jump, and he gives me a sly grin. "Sit. You will eat first then get dressed later," Roman tells me. And dang, I want to say, *"Yes, sir,"* to see what he will do.

I giggle and he raises his brow at me. "Or not... I like wearing your clothes."

He nods, grunts, and returns to the stove.

I take a seat, and Asher sits across from me. I take a sip of orange juice and it's so fresh.

"It's freshly squeezed," Hunter says as he kisses the side of my head. Then he takes a seat beside me, and I drop my head to his shoulder. God, this guy.

"I feel very spoiled."

Jace comes out of the room and squeezes my shoulder as he takes a seat beside Asher. "Get used to it. We all want to spoil you." Jace smiles and waves his hand around. "This is your life now. Hunter and Roman are here alone. Imagine if we had a place like this. This is your home, and we are your four husbands, spoiling you all the time."

I smile at the thought. Only, Hunter and Jace will go off to college. Asher too… Fuck. Roman and I will be the only two left. I'm not going to college. I have a plan, and it involves Roman.

"After four years of college for the three of you?" I quirk a brow. I want to know what his plans are. I want Jace to chase his dream. I want all of them to.

Asher shrugs. "I don't know, I have money for college, but I don't know if I'm gonna go now."

"Asher, you can't not go. You want to go, I know that. I want us to all stay together, but I know that's not going to happen, and there's nothing wrong with long distance. We will make it work. I promise." I reach over and grip his hand.

"I don't need to go to college. I can get a job doing construction. I'm good with my hands," Jace says.

I shake my head. "No, you are getting that scholarship and going to college, or you're not allowed to be my boyfriend anymore."

Jace grumbles, but I see the smile on his face. He wants college, but he doesn't want to lose me, and I'm going to make sure he knows that won't happen as many times as he needs to hear it.

"No one will break up, I promise. If you all go to college, we will work it out. Maybe if you all get into the same one, Roman and I can move close, and we can all live together."

They all nod, and Roman places the bacon, eggs, and pancakes in front of us all.

"Okay, I agree to that because Roman can cook," Asher says as he dives in.

I realize Hunter hasn't said anything, and I squeeze his leg under the table. I want to know what's going through his head.

But either way, that conversation has started, and I'm glad. It's been something I have worried about. Them changing their dreams for me.

I don't want that, and I couldn't live with myself if they did.

I see Joe's name on my caller ID and hesitate.

Asher takes it from my hand and answers. "Hi, Joe. It's Asher, Mila's boyfriend. I will just get her for you."

I put my hands up in a silent plea, mouthing the word *no*. I can't talk to him; I don't want to know. But Asher puts the cell in my hand and walks away.

Hearing Joe calling out through the speakers, I take a deep breath and still myself before I put the phone to my ear. "Hi, Joe." I grit my teeth. I don't want to know what happened with my mother. I've seen a little bit of it on the news, but I turned it off, because I just couldn't face the fact that she tried to frame me.

"Mila, I'm not sure if you heard the news, but your mother and your stepbrother have been arrested for the murder of Malcolm."

I nod and whisper, "Yes."

Joe continues. "They found Junior. He had knife wounds that were healing on his hands, and he confessed to murdering his father. Apparently, your mother and him were having an affair for the past two years. When Malcolm found out the baby wasn't his, he confronted them and demanded a divorce.

"They threatened to go to the media about it, and he didn't want that for his son or his granddaughter. It also wouldn't look good with his business partners, so you coming back to New York was so he could explain what was going to happen, and he'd hoped you would help support your mother during the transition. He'd bought an apartment in the same building for your mother to raise the baby. So his grandchild would be close and well taken care of."

I let out a sob, the tears tracking down my cheeks. Malcolm was the nicest guy. He was odd and old-fashioned at times, but he was always there. He cared, in his own way. He wasn't close to me. I wouldn't say we had a good relationship. But he was always working or doing whatever Mom wanted him to do. Like sending me away back home to Ridgecrest.

But for his own wife and son to kill him... that is so sad. He didn't have much in the way of family; his son was the only family he really had.

"Mom wanted me to come home. She wanted me to return because she knew I had killed someone in self-defense here, and it's easy to pin a murder on a murderer," I said. It wasn't a question. I'd put it all together; it's the only thing that makes sense.

"Yes, and it seems his will is going to be an issue. You're the next of kin for your mother."

My mouth dropped open. "What are you saying?" *I don't want blood money.* "I don't want Malcolm's money. I want Malcolm back. I would choose him over money any day of the week."

"You're better than most, Mila. Stay like that. The world needs more people like you. Still, you are next in line, but the baby your mother's carrying will also have a half share."

Fuck, I forgot about the poor baby. So innocent in all of this. Her parents in jail before she's even born and shit. Who will raise her? I'm too young. Dad and Kate? No.

"Junior's mom, will she raise the baby?" I ask him.

"She has asked to have custody of the baby, yes, but I wanted to discuss what you wanted to do?"

I shake my head and wipe the tears away. "No, I think she should raise her granddaughter. She wasn't a bad mom. She just had a bad egg from the start. And I don't want the money, Joe. Not one cent. I want you to give it all to the baby. She's gonna need it."

That, and a lot of therapy.

"Just tell me one thing. Am I ever gonna see either of them walking free in my lifetime?"

"No," Joe replies.

I nod and end the call while sitting there, staring at the blank wall. Asher comes back in and wraps his arms around me, and I cry. He holds me for as long as I need to let it all out.

I don't think I will get over Malcolm's death. Damon was different. He deserved what was coming to him. Malcolm... he would have made a great grandfather. I think he's one of those guys who would have spoiled his grandchild.

"Mila?" Asher whispers my name.

I haven't cried in a while, and I'm just lying in Asher's arms, thinking of all the nice things Malcolm had ever done for me. "Yeah?" I say as he rocks me softly.

"There were some Christmas gifts sent here from Joe. They're from Malcolm and your mom, but he said that Malcolm bought them, and he wanted you to have them."

I sit up and look around the room. I don't see any gifts.

"I hid them in my room. Mom said you might not be ready, and I didn't want you getting upset over them, so I have been holding onto them for you."

I rub my eyes and nod. "I want them." I do. Malcolm made every Christmas special for me. Even if he got his secretary to buy them, the gifts are still special to me.

Asher jumps up, and when he returns, he has three gifts. One is large and the other two are smaller.

"Joe spoke to his secretary..."

My brows raise, and I laugh. "I knew it. I knew she did the Christmas shopping."

Asher shakes his head at me. "No, apparently, he did it all himself. He was a huge fan of Christmas and giving. So, he would ask her where to find the things he wanted to buy you and Junior."

My face drops at the mention of Junior. But Malcolm actually bought my gifts. I swallow the lump in my throat. All the gifts he gave me were meaningful. Things I liked.

I nod and take the big gift. I remove the wrapping

paper gently, not wanting to rip it. I don't think he wrapped them—they're store wrapped—but I just don't want to rip something that he touched. When I open the box, I find watercolors and a canvas. There's a guide to watercolor painting in there too, and I suck in a breath.

I'm speechless. The lump in my throat grows larger as I pull it all out, including one of Malcolm's business cards. On the back, it says, "I believe in you, Mila," and I burst out crying.

Asher's holding me again, and I think my crying has triggered everyone in the house. Kate is by my side, and she wraps me in her arms.

Dad stands back and looks at the card. "Oh, sweetheart."

And I nod. I want to tell them what it means. What this gift means to me and why it's making me cry.

"I was walking through Central Park one day, and I saw an artist painting with watercolors. It was a beautiful painting, and I came home and told my mom and Malcolm at dinner."

I frown slightly. That dinner, Mom told me I was wasting my time with painting and that I should be spending my time finding a rich boyfriend at school.

"Mom wasn't interested in my art, ever. She didn't care, but Malcolm encouraged me. Even when she put me down, he would tell me not to listen. One of the last times I saw him before coming back here, he asked me if I still liked watercolor, and I said I gave up art. That I wasn't good enough. And he told me he believed in me. That art comes from within, and he could see I have talent."

I touch the paints with my fingertips, and Kate sniffs beside me. "I'm so sorry for your loss, Mila."

She hugs me tighter, and I realize then that no one has said that to me. I was viewed as the killer and not the victim for so long that it must not have registered that I lost him. That it was a loss to me, and people should pay their respects like they did for Roman when he lost his father.

Malcolm might not have been my father, but he was someone who meant something to me. He treated me like a person when my mother treated me like a mistake. I will make sure that baby in her tummy never knows her, and she will never know what it's like to feel less than by her own mother.

My dad moves in and wraps me in his arms, and I cry. "Malcolm was a good man. I'm sorry for your loss, sweetheart. You've had too much happen in your life already. I love you and only want you to be happy from now on."

I let out a deep sigh and yawn. I'm exhausted.

"You need some rest. How about a nap, and when you wake up, Kate and I will bake you a cake?"

I smile and nod, wanting to see how good my dad is at baking. I let him carry me to my bed. I feel like I'm five years old again.

"I love you, Dad," I whisper as he lays me down and tucks me into bed.

"I love you always, my baby girl." He kisses me on the head, and I close my eyes, letting sleep take me.

CHAPTER 15
JACE

ila's been back home for two weeks. Her mom and stepbrother have been arrested, and she's smiling more. Thank fuck, because if the cops didn't do something about them, I was gonna go to New York and find Junior. But Alessandro's guy pulled through, and they found where the slimy fucker had been hiding.

"I'm taking her on a date tonight," I tell Asher as he opens the door for me. He's dressed in shorts and a blue tee, looking completely normal. Still, it's weird to see him after watching the four of them together. It's not every day you see your girl and three other cocks.

"I know." He gives me a puzzled look. "She's still getting dressed and asked me to get the door."

I walk into the house and wave to Madison and her friend in the living room. Madison smiles and gives me a small wave, but the other girl turns beet red and stares at me.

I move on to the kitchen, where I find Kate cooking, and it smells amazing.

"Hi, Kate. Are you baking a cake?" I swear this lady's a magician when it comes to cakes, and I'm gonna get so fat just hanging around here. And I don't care; all the extra time in the gym is worth it.

"I'm currently making a chocolate mud cake. I heard you were coming over here tonight to take Mila on a date. Can I ask where you're taking her?"

I laugh. The guys have hounded me for days over the location, but I won't tell them. I don't want to spoil the surprise for Mila. Plus, I don't want them to steal my idea. Well, okay, it's my mom's idea, but still. I put my hand to my mouth and mime zipping my mouth shut.

She chuckles. "Must be somewhere very special."

I nod, although I'm not too sure Mila will find it special. I hope so because I want this to be special.

I had asked my mom what kind of date to take Mila on, and she gave me a bunch of different ideas, but the one that stood out the most was taking her on a picnic by the lake we used to swim in. Mom had said dates like that, personal ones, are a lot more romantic than taking her to some fancy restaurant and spending a heap of money. And if I prepare the food myself, that's even better.

I haven't taken a girl on a date before. Going to

the diner after school doesn't count. That's just where everyone hangs out.

I want to make this extraordinary for Mila. Want it to be a memorable night.

Last weekend, we didn't do anything but kiss, and I want this to be the night we go a little further. I like that we are taking it slow. Yeah, I'm just as surprised by that. But I feel that if we go all the way now, it will feel rushed. I've waited my whole life to be with Mila. I don't need to rush now. I'm taking my time; kissing her and cuddling her is something I'm really enjoying right now. I'm gonna marry this girl one day, and I want to start off our relationship right. I rushed with Britney, and I don't want to make that mistake again.

"Very special," I hear Mila say as she enters the room.

Her blonde hair is down and curled at the ends. She's wearing a pink tee with a pair of blue jeans and white sneakers. Her makeup's very minimal compared to when she wears a lot of dark around her eyes. I love both looks. She's always beautiful.

Mila looks like the girl next door, and she is to me. Even with her living over here now, she'll always be my girl next door.

She reaches out and takes my hand in hers, and I kiss her lips briefly. Don't want to get carried away in front of Kate. And we have a date that I don't want to be late for. The sun will set before we even get a chance to put down the blanket, and I don't want it to get too cold. I have a spare hoodie in my car, just in case she gets cold. I want her to wear mine.

"We better get going. Save me some cake." I point to the oven, and Kate smiles.

"I'm sure there will be cake when you get back. Asher and Madison are all caked out. They barely eat it anymore."

My mouth drops in a dramatic way that has Kate laughing. "No way. I volunteer as tribute. I will eat anything you bake, Kate."

Mila playfully smacks my chest, and I look down but see she's smiling and shaking her head. "I'll bake you cakes too," she says, and I kiss her nose. She rolls her eyes.

"Okay, dear. I'll eat all the cakes you bake," I tease in an old-man voice. Then I move in and pull her close to whisper, "I wanna eat your muffin."

Mila gasps and pulls away, smacking me with a shocked look on her face. I grin at her. Yeah, I do wanna eat her muffin... later.

"What happened?" Kate asks Mila, and I see that gleam in her eye. *Fuck.*

"Jace just said he wants to ea—mmm." Mila's eyes widen as my hand holds her mouth closed, and Kate just stares at us.

"I said I would eat anything she bakes. We better go now. Bye." I don't let go of Mila's mouth as I direct her out of the kitchen.

She waves to Kate, and Asher eyes us as we move past him.

"Hey, not so fast." James's voice is deep, coming from the living room. Ah, fuck.

She better not be rude to her dad. I stop and look over at him. He eyes my hand and Mila's eyes, which are smiling. I don't think he knows what to say. I haven't taken my hand off her mouth, and after a few seconds, he nods. "Have a good night you two. Don't be home late."

"Ah, I was wondering if it was okay with you... My mom and dad said it was okay that Mila stays at my house?" I give him my all-American, boy-next-door smile. The one that works on everyone, *except James*. His eyes narrow, and I take a small step back. Fuck, he knows I hurt her and made her cry. He hasn't forgiven me yet. She's allowed to stay at Hunter's without parents and mine are actually home.

He points at me, and I stand straighter. I'm ready for whatever he's going to say. "You sleep on the couch," he states, and I nod and swallow.

Why did that make me so nervous? Maybe because this is our first real date?

"Yes, sir. Of course. I was going to sleep with Grady."

He eyes me again, and Mila's shoulders are shaking with laughter. Why?

"Night. Have fun, baby girl." Then he winks

at her.

I take my hand from her mouth, and she giggles before running over and hugging him. "Night, Dad. Come on. Let's go, Jace." She takes my hands and drags me out of the house.

Is he playing me? What the hell just happened? I'm so confused.

I glance to Mila, and she has a huge grin on her face. "He was fucking with me. Wasn't he?"

She gives me a cheeky wink and lets go of my hand as she runs to my car.

My car that was impounded and has acquired an insane number of miles after its trip to New York and back again. It got a scratch and dent, but I never mentioned it. I don't care about the car, just that it brought two very important people back to me.

I park at the lake and Mila eyes me warily.

"The lake? You're not gonna push me in, are you?" She cocks a brow at me.

I hadn't been expecting her to say that. "No?" Her brows rise as she purses her lips—fuck. "Sorry, I mean, no. I won't push you in. Why would you think I would?"

"You told me that all the time when we were down here as kids. Seeing the rope swing... it just reminded me of that. Of the happy times down here when life was less complicated."

Shit, should I have picked a different spot to take her? I didn't want her to get upset over the memories. But, shit. They were some of my favorite memories of us.

"If it was warm enough, I might push you in, but it's not. So, I promise not to push you in."

She laughs and gets out the car, and I follow her out. The sounds of frogs and the wind blowing through the tress make this spot perfect. We're away from houses here, so it's quiet. I round my car and get out the blanket and picnic basket, filled with food I made.

"Oh my god, Jace. A picnic?" she squeals, and I smile.

I knew this was the right choice for the date. I walk down to the water's edge and place the blanket on the ground. Mila finds a few rocks and throws them into the lake, and I take a seat on the blanket.

It's chilly, but I'll go back for the hoodie when she needs it. She can come snuggle me for warmth.

"You know what? This place looks so much smaller now. Now that we're all grown up, everything around us has shrunk. Like all the fun stuff left too. All the things we did as kids. I miss that. Carefree fun. We need to come back here in summer when it's hot enough to swim."

I smile over at her as she throws another rock into

the murky water. The sun's setting and is streaking the sky with pink, oranges, and reds. It's absolutely perfect. Apart from the chill in the air, this is the best date.

"Everyone grew up, and those things were childish, Mila. But I miss them too. Remember when we caught that frog and let it out in my house?"

Mila bursts out laughing, and I do too. "Your mom was so freaked out."

I snort. Mom was so mad at us.

She comes over and sits beside me. I wrap my arm over her shoulder, and we stare out to the dark lake. The colors in the sky are just perfect as we sit here together and watch the sky.

"Remember that one summer when I said I couldn't swim because I hurt myself, and you would carry me on your back? I think we were ten?"

I smile and murmur, "Yes."

"I wasn't actually injured. I just had a huge crush on you that summer and wanted to be hugging you heaps." She giggles, and I sit back to look at her. Her skin is so beautiful in the light of the sunset. Her eyes shine bright as she tilts her head slightly. "It was the only excuse I could come up with for hugging you. And it worked."

"I wish you had told me back then. I loved having to carry you everywhere. You told Roman and Hunter that it had to be me, and I felt so special. Like I was your favorite."

Her smile falters a little, and I touch her chin with my thumb. "Don't stop smiling. You chose me, and that's all that matters. The others feel the same. We all feel like the favorite because you chose us. It was always gonna be this way... and, well, Asher." She rolls her eyes, and I put my hand up. "Hey, I get it. He's charming... bit of a dick. But he has appeal."

She smacks my chest. "Jace, don't say mean things about my boyfriend, especially when you've also been a bit of a dick in the past. We're leaving all that shit in the past. So no bringing up dicks. Cause I've seen yours and, well..." She holds her thumb and forefinger up an inch apart.

"No way. You know that's not true." I pin her to the blanket and straddle her waist. "Tell me I have the world's biggest dick."

She shakes her head and giggles. "It's tiny. So small, I can't even see it."

I take her hand and place it over my cock, which is growing hard from just being around Mila.

"Mmm... is that an ant's dick?"

"Oh, you asked for it." I tickle her sides like I used to, and her squeal of laughter echoes around us.

But I don't let up. "Say, 'Jace has a big dick.'"

She squirms under me in a fit of giggles as I get her in all her most ticklish spots. "No," she giggles. "Stop." More giggles. "Jace..."

I stop, and she lets out a deep breath. I raise my brows, and she gives me that sly grin before rocking her hips. My cock grows harder, and I rock it against her so she can feel it. What she does to me.

"Your tiny ant dick is tickling me," she says, then she giggles like crazy.

I tickle her until she can't giggle anymore. I let up, and she lies there, under me, breathing rapidly from all that laughter. So glad to hear it.

Fuck, if we're out here, being honest, I need to tell her something. "Remember when someone took your teddy... the cute one with the moon on its belly that you slept with at night?"

"Yes?" she asks, but I think she knows where I'm going with this.

God, I hope she forgives me. "I want to get this out in the open. And please don't hate me. But I stole it."

Her mouth drops open, and she pushes me off her so she can sit up. I miss her touch already. "You stole Bedtime Bear?"

I nod. Her mouth drops open again.

"Why? I loved him, and I slept with him every night. Until he disappeared and my dad said I must have lost him. But I never took him from my bed."

"I know and I'm sorry." I feel guilty as hell, but I wanted to tell her my crush story after she told me about her crush story. "I fell in love with you, Mila. From the first day I understood what love meant. And I was so scared to tell you. Scared that you might laugh at me, so I didn't. Instead, I stole your bear and slept with it every night for months until it stopped smelling like you. And even then... I still slept with it."

She stares at me, dumbfounded. Because, yeah, it was a dick move. Mila even cried when she couldn't find her bear, and I was going to give it back, but her dad bought her the one with the rainbow on its tummy, and she was happy again.

"You even helped me look for it."

I nod guiltily. I did that. "I'm not proud of myself. I was young, but it was still a dick move. What I'm trying to say is... I have been making dick moves for a long time, and if I make another in the future, please forgive me. You make me crazy, Mila. I love you so much that I stole your teddy."

"I love you, Jace."

She kisses me, and I take her hair and gather it up as I kiss her deeper, nipping her lips and chasing her tongue with mine. She pulls away, and my heart races just from that kiss. *Fuck*. I'm so glad she came back home and that she took us all as hers.

"Do you still have Bedtime Bear? Do you still sleep with him?"

I chuckle. "No, I don't sleep with him now. But I do have him. As if I could ever let him go. Even when I was mad at you, I kept him. He has a place at the back of my closet. He hides, mostly because my mom looked for him in my room when your dad told her about his disappearance. I guess she suspected me. Hell, I didn't do that good of a job. I was the only one who had access to your room that weekend. But then your dad got you the rainbow one, and you stopped looking."

She tilts her head and smiles. Her big blue eyes peer up at me through her lashes, and my heart skips a beat. *Gorgeous.*

"Your mom bought me the Cheer Bear, Jace. Not my dad." She shakes her head and grins. "She said she couldn't find a Bedtime one."

"Why would my mom do that?" I hid that thing so good so she couldn't find him, and at night, I would bring him out and sleep with him then hide him in the morning.

"She told me not to tell you she bought it for me. Honestly, at the time, I thought you would be jealous that she got it for me, but... oh my god, Jace. She knew. She so knew you stole him."

My mouth drops open. She knew? And she didn't tell James or Mila? She let me have the silly bear anyway. My mom must really love me, because it seriously was a dick move. Mila cried that first night. I felt so bad.

"Let's eat. I'm hungry." Mila opens the picnic basket, and my stomach drops when I see I didn't have the lid completely on the water bottle and the whole inside of the basket—well, the plastic bucket I used as a basket—is all wet and so are the sandwiches.

"Fuck." Worst date ever. How did I not see that wasn't on properly? I spent so long making those sandwiches.

She runs her hand over my cheek, and I look into her eyes. "It's okay, I love it. You made me a picnic. We can just lay here a while and then go get some burgers on the way home."

I nod, still upset with myself for ruining the picnic. A little ant walks over Mila's finger, and she giggles, holding it up to me.

"Look, I found your dick."

CHAPTER 16
MILA

We arrive back at Jace's place, and he takes my hand as he walks me in. His dad's there and stands up to greet me. This is the first time I have seen him since we became an official couple. He said his parents don't get the whole *four boyfriends* thing, but they love me and him. And the boys.

"Mila, it's so good to see you." Daniel wraps his arms around me and gives me a hug.

"Good to see you too, Daniel."

Ella squeals when she sees me, dropping a plate of homemade cookies on the coffee table and extracting me from Daniel so she can hug me. I love her so much. She was a mother to me for most of my childhood, and I will always love her for that.

"Mom, can I ask you why you bought Mila a Care Bear?"

Ella pulls away from me and looks up at her son. We both do. "What bear?" she questions.

"You know, the rainbow one. After my Bedtime Bear went missing, you gave it to me and told me not to tell Jace."

Her eyes widen and she looks to Daniel, who shakes his head and sits down. He has a funny look on his face, like he doesn't want to talk about this.

"Yes, I did. I saw you had stolen it, Jace."

I turn to him and point. "I told you that's why. She knew you had my bear and replaced mine and let you keep Bedtime Bear." Which is total crap. They should have given him a new bear. Bedtime Bear was mine. But then, I loved my Cheer Bear just as much in the end. Mostly because Ella bought it for me.

"But why didn't you just give it back?" he asks his mom, and that's when I see Ella's cheeks turn pink.

Oh shit. I glare at Jace. He wouldn't have... would he?

"What were you doing with my bear at night?" I poke him.

He looks between us, a confused look on his face. Then his mouth drops open. "I wasn't fucking the bear."

No one says a thing, and the silence is deafening.

"Oh god, is that what you both think?" He groans, pulling his hair.

I hear Daniel clear his throat. "That's what we all

thought, Jace. We told James what happened, and your mother replaced the bear because we all thought you were… *loving it*."

I feel like I'm in some funny prank show, only this one's even better, because I know the guy. I look at everyone, trying to work out what the heck just happened. My dad, Ella, and Daniel all thought Jace was fucking my bear? I try to hide my smile, but that shit is so embarrassing and funny.

"I wasn't *loving* the bear, Dad. *Oh god*. I was in love with Mila, and I wanted to keep something of hers close to me. I can tell you right now, that bear has not been touched by my junk. At all." Jace paces, and it's obvious he's embarrassed as all hell. Hell, I feel for him… a little.

I smirk. "Well, I would hope so. Bedtime Bear can't consent. I want him back, and he better be jizz free."

Daniel lets out a snort, and I turn to see his hand over his mouth while he looks anywhere but at us. Ella makes a sound in the back of her throat and shakes her head, trying not to laugh at her poor son, who's standing there, defending himself against sexual acts he may or may not have committed against my teddy bear.

Jace eyes me, and I can tell he's getting worked up. I put my hands up and wave a white flag… metaphorically, of course. His shoulders sag, and I reach out and take his hand.

"It's okay. I never thought you were fucking my teddy bear."

He rolls his eyes, but then he sighs. His posture settles and he calms down. Sometimes, you can push him and he doesn't snap. Other times, his aggression comes out fast and free without him ever realizing. Then he regrets his words and gets angry for being angry and it's a vicious cycle. So, before it starts, I squeeze his hand, wave to Ella—and the cookies calling my name—and lead Jace up the stairs, past Grady, who's grinning and shaking his head.

"Don't you dare." I point a finger in Grady's face and try not to smile but fail miserably.

Grady tightens his lips to hide the grin. I snort and kiss his cheek. Once we're in the room with the door closed behind us, I relax.

"You're not gonna tell the guys what happened down there, right?" Jace pleads.

I look anywhere but at Jace—his dirty clothes pile all over the floor, his bed, which isn't made... the tissues and lube. My mouth drops open and I point to it. "Okay, I won't tell them, but I will tell them about your happy tissues."

He looks over and his eyes widen. I giggle as he groans and quickly moves toward it all. "Nothing is going right tonight." He puts the lube into a drawer before picking up the tissues and tossing them in the trash.

"I think everything has gone just right. I'm about

to get back my Bedtime Bear, and you're gonna cuddle me while we watch a movie. And if you're lucky... you won't be needing tissues tonight."

His eyes widen at that, and I jump on his bed and move up so I'm sitting right in the middle against the headboard. I know he mentioned taking it slow, which I love, but there are no rules about hands and mouths.

And I can't wait to get my hands on him. I swear, with all the guys, I'm always horny.

Jace doesn't waste time. He reaches into his closet and pulls out a very sad looking blue teddy.

I frown at it. "Are you sure you didn't *love* love him? He looks very loved to me."

He grunts. I bet he wants to tell me to shut up, but he doesn't. I beam, holding my hands out so I can cuddle my teddy bear. He passes it to me then shuffles onto the bed beside me. He places his head on my belly and wraps his arm around me.

"I loved him, but not in that way. I love you more."

Jace settles down beside me, scrolling through Netflix, trying to find something. I swear we spend more time scrolling than actually watching movies. We can't decide what to watch, and he always picks superhero movies. He suggests we play video games, but I don't want to. I want to snuggle.

"Okay, it's my choice and I pick... *Ted*."

Jace rolls his eyes at my choice of a teddy bear

movie, and I laugh. But he puts it on, and we settle down together in the dark room, me curled up at his side and his arm around me as he rubs his thumb over my skin. I hold my old teddy and laugh at the silly movie with Jace. The moment's perfect. There's nothing we're running from, no one chasing us, no one looking for us. We're just two regular teens watching a movie after a sweet date.

This is the way it should have been when I came back at the start of junior year. Easy, sweet, and loving.

There's a knock at the door. Ella opens it and pops her head around the corner. She has a grin on her face. I think she likes me being with Jace. I guess they all thought we would end up together eventually, even if they did think he was fucking my teddy bear. I need to tell my dad when I get home. I don't want him thinking Jace was doing things to my stuffed toy.

"Night, you two. Don't stay up too late."

I give her a small wave and hold up Bedtime Bear, and Jace grumbles something incoherent. She just laughs, obviously understanding his language. I understand it too. It's, "Mom, leave—you're cramping my style."

The movie goes on into the night, and I can't keep my eyes open. I feel safe and warm with Jace beside me, and I fall asleep in his arms.

I wake to Jace's warm body pressed against me. He pulled the covers over me at some point during the night. I'd lost the jeans too... Well, I don't remember that part; he must have taken them off. I'm just wearing my underwear and the tee and bra I had on the night before.

Jace is only wearing his boxers, and he's hard... everywhere. I smile lazily as I arch my back, my arm reaching back, snaking around Jace's neck to pull him closer.

A large, calloused hand wraps around my middle and pulls me even closer to that hard body, grinding his erection on my ass, and I chuckle.

"Good morning," he murmurs into my hair, and my heart beats just a little faster. It is a good morning, waking up next to Jace.

Tipping my head back, I open my eyes, and two big brown ones peer down at me. Jace's hair is a mess rather than its usual styled 'do, and it's so cute. I want to reach up and mess it up more.

It's still dark in his room, but I feel so awake. That was the best sleep I've had this week. No nightmares.

"What time is it?" I look out his window, and it's still dark out. He really needs to close the curtains, even though no one is looking in from next door. Dad said he was going to rent the place out to a teacher who just moved here.

"Well... it's five a.m."

"Why are we waking up so early?" I groan. That's crazy early for me.

He gives me that stupid grin of his that makes my body tingle. Fucker. He grinds his erection into my ass again. "I didn't turn off my alarm, but I thought I was quick enough not to wake you."

"What kind of psycho sets their alarm for five a.m.?"

He chuckles, and I realize it's for him to get up and train. He gets up early and runs, hits the gym, and works out. *Every day.*

"I don't often get to wake up next to you, so this is a nice way to wake up today. I could get used to this."

I smile. *Me too.*

His fingers trail along my bare leg, and the feeling makes my nipples harden and strain against the bra I'm still wearing. I hate sleeping in a bra.

God, Jace is good at this, I think as he teases my inner thigh, so close to where I want him to touch me but dancing away at the last second. I can feel myself growing wet from his little moves.

This boy-next-door knows how to kiss and how to play my body. His fingers move up my thigh, higher, until his hand is on my waist and slips under the fabric. I shift to give him more access to where I want him to touch me.

I need this so bad. He hesitates for a moment before kissing me. I'm surprised when his thumb brushes over my clit, having not felt his hand move. I moan into his mouth and I can feel him smile.

"We have to be quiet," he whispers.

I smirk. Like I can be quiet. I'm so used to being at Hunter's without anyone to overhear us—other than Jace—that I forget how to be quiet.

"You might need to help me." Because this is what we have been inching toward all week, and I want to taste him. I want him to make me come. But I know I can't be quiet while he does all those things.

I feel him silently laughing and he kisses my nose. "Trust me, I want you to scream my name for the guys to hear how much I please you, but not my parents."

I grin. Between the games and running races at Hunter's, the guys are always competing. They haven't turned the challenge of who can please me the best into a contest yet. I'll have to drop a hint or two and reap the rewards.

He shuffles away, removing his hand from my underwear, and I make a sad sound at the loss of touch.

"Greedy girl, I want to taste you. I want you coming on my tongue, Mila."

I swallow and the butterflies return to my belly. Yeah, I'm not going to complain about that.

I pull off my tee, and he helps me with my bra, my breasts spilling free and aching to be touched.

"Fuck, your tits are perfect, Mila."

I throw the sheets back and he looks down at me, biting his lower lip into his mouth and nodding. I'm lying on his bed, only wearing my panties, and he's looking at me like he won the lottery. Like he's the luckiest guy on earth. And I feel like I won the same lottery when it comes to him. He makes me feel so sexy.

My scars from the car accident are healed and faded, but he runs his fingers over the larger one on my side before he leans over and kisses it.

Those deep brown eyes of his watch me. He's stunning. There's no denying that. He knows it too, which make him a little cocky, but I love that about him. His sure-of-himself attitude is something he didn't have when I left almost five years ago. But it's here now, and I'm ready for it.

"While you're down there, kissing me…"

His brows raise, but I see that smirk. He knows what I need, but he comes up and kisses my lips. My jaw. My throat.

Jace traces his tongue along my collarbone and down my breast before sucking my nipple into his mouth. *Fuck.* I bow off the bed as he swirls his tongue around, and my body responds. I grip his bed hair, my hips bucking up, trying to find some friction.

My nipple pops free, and as he blows over it, it tightens, and it feels amazing. He chuckles as I try to pull him closer to do the same to the other.

"Tease," I mumble.

He gives the other some quick attention before dropping between my legs and kissing and licking. His tongue sends the most amazing tingles of pleasure to my core, but he's still not where I want him. My hands still in his hair, I press for him to get closer to where I want his tongue on me.

He looks up at me as he kisses my pussy over my underwear. They're so wet and he inhales my scent. *Fuck.*

"Someone is a little impatient."

I groan. He needs to know what I think about his teasing. "If you're just gonna tease me, I will have to call someone who knows how to take care of my needs." I fake going for my phone, and he lunges for it, snapping it up.

I have woken that beast inside him—the jealous one. Yes, I poked it. But it's so worth it to see the way he looks down at me like he wants to mark me as his for all to see.

He cocks his head, and he takes a photo of me sprawled out on his bed. I watch as he taps on the screen, and then his eyes darken and he growls in the back of his throat, sending shivers down my spine... the best kind.

"Is this what you want?" He pulls on my underwear, and it snaps at the waist. My mouth drops open, but his eyes are full of need... of want to claim me.

The phone moves with him, and I think he's

recording me, but I don't care. I want him to take me now. I reach for his cock, but he shakes his head. "You need to learn patience, Mila."

I flop back down, and he grins. It's not the boy-next-door smile anymore. This grin is dark and dirty, promising me wicked things are about to come.

I shake my head and poke my tongue out at him. I don't need to learn patience; he needs to learn to hurry up and give me what I want.

Jace lowers his face and presses a soft kiss between my thighs, his hot breath setting me off. My body shivers at the pleasure I got just from that one kiss.

"Fuck," I moan, grabbing the pillow and pulling it to my face.

I have to be quiet, but I know I can't. Not with the way Jace already has me worked up. He drops the phone beside me, and I see that he has started a video chat with the guys but muted them so we can't hear them. Hunter's lying in bed, shirtless, wearing his black-rimmed glasses, and he looks tired. Roman's watching in the dark. I can't see him, but I know he's listening, and Asher hasn't even picked up. Which makes me want to laugh. He sleeps in whenever he can, and he's missing the show.

It's funny that Jace called them, because he won't touch me like this when they're in the room. But he has them here... watching us through my phone.

Maybe he needs this as the first step toward group fun.

"Fuck, Mila," Jace rumbles, and my legs spread farther apart as my core clenches around nothing, wanting to be filled. "You have the most perfect pussy."

He swipes his tongue over my slit, and I moan, gripping the pillow to my mouth as I watch him.

His eyes never leave mine. "Your taste is intoxicating." He spreads me wider, licking and sucking on my clit. My hands grip the pillow as my body bows off the bed, wanting him closer, then the feeling becomes too much and I'm backing away. But he won't let me. His grip is tight on my thigh as he keeps me where he wants.

The pleasure hits me, and I tumble over the edge into an intense orgasm, my legs shaking. He doesn't let up; he chases the orgasm with his tongue, not letting me have a chance to come down from the high as I ride the wave. Two fingers plunge into my soaking heat, and I clutch the pillow, trying so hard to keep quiet. But my breathing is heavy and loud. Everyone in the house will know what we are doing in here if they walk past Jace's room.

When his fingers find my G-spot, my core clenches around him, sucking him deeper as he fucks me with his skilled fingers and licks my clit with his tongue. His eyes never leave mine, watching my reactions as I gasp. I bite the pillow as I call out his name, coming around his fingers. Still, he doesn't let up, fucking me until the orgasm has all but left me with just aftershocks remaining.

"Jace," I pant, trying to catch my breath.

He grins, and this time, it's the boy-next-door grin, and my core clenches around his fingers again. Holy shit. I can hardly breathe. "You looked so good coming around my fingers." He moves up my body and kisses me.

Tasting myself on his lips, I moan. "I want more." I reach for his boxers, and he stills my hand, his expression changing back to the dark and dirty Jace.

"Get down on your knees," he growls into my ear, and I shiver.

Oh fuck, this is going to get interesting. He's very controlling in the bedroom. Not like Hunter... This isn't a question or a suggestion. This is a demand. And I'm so here for it.

I crawl off the bed, and Jace follows, the phone coming with him. He aims it down his body so the others can see me looking up at him and his cock straining against his boxers.

Jace is kinkier than I thought. He doesn't like to share, but he wants them to see what he does to me and what I do to him.

I lick my lips as the butterflies grow.

I'm ready for the dark side of Jace Montero.

CHAPTER 17
JACE

This is it. Where I ask her to trust me. Mila is safe—I know that. She would never judge me for my tastes. I see how she is with the guys; I get jealous of them together. I want to join in, but I want to have Mila for my own. On another level, I want the control that I can't have in group sex.

Hunter was calling the shots, but not in a way I would. He suggests things, making sure everyone is safe and comfortable.

I respect him for that, but right now, I want Mila to swallow my cock whole. I want to grab her hair and fuck her pretty little mouth. I don't want to be gentle. I want to make love to her... but not now. Now's not the time. I'm too worked up to do it slow and gentle, which I know she deserves. I want to teach her how I like my cock sucked.

I like the control or, at least, the fantasy of it. I'm gonna show Mila and the guys. I want them to understand this is me. I haven't explored this as much as I've wanted, but I know how I like my cock sucked, and I want Mila to like that too.

Mila goes for my boxers, but I let out a deep rumble in my chest, and her eyes widen. Her hands go to her lap, and I smile down at her while brushing my thumb over her jaw.

"Do you trust me?" I ask and she nods. "Trust I won't hurt you?"

"Yes, Jace."

My chest swells. I know I'm not asking for something crazy of her, but I want her trust that I won't go too far. I know my girl is good at sucking cock; I watched her last week. But what I want, it isn't gentle.

I can see on the phone's screen that Hunter's wearing his glasses and is very awake. Asher's watching closely, and Roman's still in the dark. But I know he's watching my every move.

"Take out my cock."

She looks up at me through her lashes, and I bite my lip to stop myself from moaning. Fuck, she's perfect. As she tugs the waistband down and my cock springs free, she licks her lips and watches it against my stomach. But she doesn't touch. She's waiting for me to tell her.

She might have been teasing earlier about how

big I am, but she knows. I'm longer than Hunter. I'm thicker than Asher... but, fuck. Roman. His cock's a monster.

"Open your mouth," I growl.

Holding the base of my cock, I see movement on the screen, but I ignore them and watch as Mila opens her mouth, sticking her tongue out. Fuck, she knows what I want before I even ask it. Has she done this before? I growl deep in my chest at the thought, and she doesn't move. I narrow my eyes at her, but she doesn't shift.

"Good girl," I praise her as I rub my cock head against her cheek, tapping her tongue a few times.

She moans but keeps her mouth open as I dip my cock into her warm mouth. She swallows as I press in deeper, and when I feel her gag, I pull back. I know where her limit is. I might like control, but I don't like to push it past there. That's not for me. I want her to enjoy this too.

"Suck me."

Her lips wrap around my cock, and I let go, grabbing a fistful of her hair and working her mouth. She goes deeper and deeper until she's almost at the base, and I can feel myself fucking her throat. *Holy shit.* I'm about to come, but I want to play this out a little longer. I had no idea she could take me that deep without gagging.

I pull back and watch her as my cock pops free, all shiny and wet from her mouth. I lick my lips and let go of her hair to swipe my thumb over her lower lip. She sucks it, and I moan. *Fuck.* This girl. Last time she had my cock, all she did was swipe my pre-cum, and I fucking came. It's so hard to hold back now. I want this to last longer than a minute, but those eyes... I swear she's trying to kill me with another orgasm without touching me.

"Behave," I warn her, and she smirks up at me. I bite the inside of my mouth. She's playing with me now, and I fucking love it. She wouldn't be Mila if she wasn't.

"Open."

She opens her mouth again and sits on her hands so she doesn't touch me. Fuck, she's perfect. I grab her hair again and direct her to my cock.

"Take me as deep as you can go."

And she does. I let out a deep groan as I try to hold the phone steady. But in the end, I give up. I throw the phone on the bed and stroke her face with my other hand as I fuck her perfect mouth.

"Fuck, so good, Mila."

Her big blue eyes are on mine as my balls tighten and I know I'm about to come.

"I'm gonna come," I warn her, giving her the choice to pull away or to let me come in her mouth.

She sucks harder, and that's enough to push me over the edge. My cock unloads into her mouth, and she doesn't let up. My body trembles and explodes with pleasure.

I pull from her mouth, and when she licks me off her lips, I shudder from the sight. Yanking her up, I grab her chin and slam my mouth against hers, tasting myself on her lips as our tongues collide. It's not gentle… I'm claiming her mouth.

She's mine.

I pull back and look down at her pink cheeks, her perfect rosebud lips, and her crazy wild hair.

"Mine," I growl before I take her mouth again.

We end up wrapped up in the sheets, holding each other. Mila talks to the guys as they work out what we're going to do for the day. Although she doesn't mention the teddy incident from last night, she cuddles her Bedtime Bear under her arm, and it's cute. She used to sleep like that with him, then I stole him.

I do feel bad. I shouldn't have taken it. I just loved her so much I wanted to be close to her… in a dumb way, I now see. But I was a dumb kid back then. Puberty got me all messed up, and I didn't know how to tell my best friend that I loved her and wanted to kiss her.

Now, I squeeze her tighter and she snuggles in closer to me. I got the girl. I have the best friends… and Asher. The guy is growing on me. I might not be his best friend yet, but it will come.

Mila picked us all. Every one of us became friends

because of her, and I trust her judgment. She hasn't picked a bad friend yet. Roman was tough; he had a real chip on his shoulder. Hunter was easy; he was sweet and shy. Me... well, I was the neighbor. She didn't exactly pick me. I picked her and she let me into her world.

"What are you thinking about so hard over there?" she asks, the phone screen now dark.

"Just life, you. Us. All of us," I mumble. She smiles at me, and I kiss her nose. "We all give you butterflies. Just funny how we all fit. How you picked us all, not realizing that, one day, we would all be yours."

She smiles and traces her finger over my brow. "I knew that you were all mine."

I chuckle. Of course, she did. When Mila has her mind and heart on something, she won't give up until it's hers.

"You know what you want, babe, and you take it. Like being friends with Roman. I never saw that working out, but you didn't give up. Or the time you learned to skateboard. You did it, even though you fell more than you rode. You want something, you go for it. You get it."

"My skateboarding skills weren't the best, but I didn't fall that much."

I chuckle and she slaps my arm.

"Oh, remember when we found that stray kitten?"

I nod and squeeze her. "We only found that little feral kitten because you fell off the skateboard, Mila."

"Well, shut up. I loved that feral little kitten, and I wanted to keep it, but my mom was allergic. So Dad had to take it to the shelter, so there. I don't get everything."

I hum in response. I remember that day. Mila was so cute, loving on that little feral kitten and never giving up. She was all scratched up, and her dad freaked out it might have rabies.

"It was trying to claw you to death," I remind her.

She just sighs. "It was scared and all alone. Anyone would do that."

It reminded me of how she was with Roman. He was scared and alone, and she kept loving him until he stopped pushing back. That kitten just needed a week with Mila, and it would have snuggled up with her. That's just how Mila is—she cares so much. Biggest heart of anyone I know.

We sit quietly, and I realize now how much that kitten meant to her, if only for a day. She wanted that little feral ball of fur. Growing up, we didn't have pets. My parents said we couldn't afford to feed them, and now they want to travel more. Roman never had a chance at a pet; he needed all his energy to take care of himself. Hunter was the only one of us that had one—his dog, Chewy, who passed away a few years back. But Mila always wanted a cat. I have no idea why, she just wanted one.

I want to get her one. A little ball of fur to make her smile. Mila's going to have everything she wants. I'm going to make sure of it.

"Do you like little white balls of fur? Or those weird naked cats?" I ask, wanting to get more information from her.

She giggles. "They're not naked. But, yeah, I don't really like those. My neighbor, when I lived in New York, had one of those fluffy white Ragdoll cats with the color on its nose and paws. I like those. They are so cute and sweet."

Ragdoll... The heck? Okay, need to remember it to Google later.

"Bet it was cute. Just like you." I tickle her, trying to distract her from talking about cats and kittens.

Hunter has a special gift for her for Christmas and is still waiting to give it to her. He forgot, then Mila went into that tailspin from Malcolm's gifts, so we all held off. Roman says he has one. I don't know what it is. Asher doesn't have a clue what to get her, and now I have the best gift idea.

A cute, fluffy kitten.

CHAPTER 18
MILA

*T*hree *months later.*

A number I don't recognize flashes on my phone screen. Sitting up, I rub my eyes and clear my throat. It's the middle of the night, and I don't know who would be calling me at this hour. Unless it's someone from New York.

"Hello?" My voice croaks from being woken up.

"Mila? Is that you, love?"

I sit up a little straighter at the female voice. "Yes?" I don't know what she's going to say, and I'm a little bit nervous. Is this about the case? Is this a reporter, trying to get a story on me? On Mom and Junior? Fucking hell, how did she get this number?

"Hi, love. It's Gail."

I don't speak for a few moments. It's Gail. Malcolm's ex-wife and Junior's mom. Why is she calling me in the middle of the night?

"I'm Junior's mom," she adds, as though I don't already know who she is. I guess I paused for a lot longer than I realized.

"Hi, Gail, I know. Sorry, you woke me up. It's like —" I look down at the caller ID. Shit, it's 3:09 a.m. Unless Mom…

"She had the baby?" I rush out, hearing Gail talking to someone in the background before responding to me.

"Sorry, love. Was just talking with a nurse. Your mom had the baby. About thirty minutes ago. A healthy baby girl. Congratulations, big sister."

I let out a deep breath and smile. I'm glad she's healthy and safe. This baby girl will have a lot of challenges in her life. But she has Gail, who I know will do anything for this little girl. She has me too. Although I'm far from her, I will do everything I can for this little girl.

"I will be taking her home in a few days. I will send you some photos, and now that you have my number, you can call anytime you want to see her or talk to me about how she is. Or if you just want to talk about anything, I would love for you to call me. We never spoke much, and I'm sorry for all that you went through with my son. But I would like us to be friends."

"I would really like that, Gail. I know you will be an amazing grandma to her. Joe told me about the property up north, away from the city, and everything that's there. I love that for her already. I grew up in a small town, and it's the best place for her to be."

Joe had called and asked if Gail could use a small portion of the money to buy a house in a cute little town, far away from the city and everything that's poison there. I told him that I would be sad if she didn't. The city is no place to raise a little girl who already had a tragic past before she was even born. The media knows about Mom, Junior, and the baby, and I would hate for her to be subjected to the scandal while growing up.

"I want to thank you so much for letting me have custody and for everything you've already given this sweet, innocent baby. You're already the best big sister this little girl could ever ask for. But you should have kept some money for yourself, so I asked Joe to help me put a portion of it into an account for you. To help put you through college, buy a first house… I know Malcolm would have wanted that for you. He spoke so highly of you and your artwork."

Joe helped her put money into an account for me? I shake my head and hold back the tears. I didn't want the money. It didn't feel right taking it. That's why I gave it all to the baby.

I change the subject; I don't want to tell her to take it back. Now isn't the time. "What did Mom name her?" I've been dreading this. Mom might be a bitch and give her some terrible name. My dad named me, thankfully. I hold my breath, waiting for Gail to tell me.

"Actually, your mother refuses to name her unless she's set free. I'm glad she chose not to. I would love if you'd help name her with me. I think it would be lovely that her big sister named her."

I hold my throat, my emotions already swelling. I can't believe Mom wouldn't name her. Well, I can. She's not a mother. And I need to remember that. *Amber*. Just a name without meaning. She's not my mother.

"Can we not call her my mother anymore? She isn't mine, and she isn't this sweet little baby's mom, either. But I would love to help name her. Thank you for asking."

"Of course. I will call that woman Amber from now on when I speak about her. Not that we need to talk about her much. But I understand—she was never a mother to you. Not a real one, and I'm sorry I didn't know that until now."

I nod into the phone, not knowing what to say.

So Gail continues, "Kate is a wonderful step-mom. I met her while all the—" She clears her throat. "I met her in the city, and we had lunch one day. She spoke so much about you and how sweet you are to her daughter Madison, befriending her instantly and helping her with her friend and the bullies at school. And she said her son Asher has never smiled as much as he has once you came along. She told me how beautiful you are as a person, and I'm sorry I didn't get to spend much time with you in the past. But I hope to spend a lot more time getting to know you and the person that you are."

I blush. I can't believe Kate said those things to Gail. I feel a lump in my throat, and I want to cry at how special Kate is to me. I'm so grateful she isn't upset with me about my relationship with Asher. I didn't think I would get this emotional over a phone call. A sweet phone call.

I clear my throat and blink away tears. "Is there someone special who was in Malcolm's life? Like his mom? He would have made a wonderful grandfather to her. So maybe something along those lines?"

"Oh, that is such a sweet idea. He had a sister who passed away when she was seven. He didn't talk about her much, but I know he loved her dearly."

Well, that doesn't help keep the tears back. That's so sad. She was so young.

"What was her name?" I ask. *Please don't be weird and old-fashioned like Malcolm.* Like, Malcolm was a cool name... for him. But I wouldn't name a child that. A middle name, yes. But not a first name.

"Her name was Lillian."

I smile. "It's a beautiful name. I think it's perfect." I sob, and I don't know why I'm crying. I think I'm just so happy that the baby is here and she's safe and I know she will be well taken care of. And emotional because Malcolm won't ever see her grow up... and neither will his sister, who died so young. But they will both be remembered through a very special little girl.

"I think so too, and I think it's a special name Malcolm would have loved. What about Hope for a middle name? Because she's a little bit of hope at the end of all of this. Lillian Hope Bradshaw."

Fuck... she has Junior's last name. I don't know how I feel about that; I know it was Malcolm's too. But still. I hope people don't put the names together and work out who her mom and dad really are.

"Gail, I think Lillian Hope is the perfect name. So much meaning behind those names. She is going to be amazing and do amazing things. I just know it."

"Me too, Mila. And with you in her life, I know she will succeed. Her big sister is already the strongest person I know. And I know, together, we will raise a very strong, independent girl."

"Thank you for calling and telling me, Gail. And I will look out for the photos you send me. I'm excited to see her."

"Bye, Mila. And call me anytime, day or night… I will be up late for the next eighteen years." She laughs and I chuckle at that.

I hang up the phone, and only moments later, images come through from Gail.

Lillian Hope. Born on the twenty-fourth of April at 5:30 a.m.

And she looks just like me. Blonde hair, so pale you can hardly see it. But with big, dark eyes. She's beautiful. I start crying. Lillian is perfect.

Amber's a bitch for not even naming her. Gail is amazing and holding it together really well, considering her son is going to prison for killing his dad. Her ex-husband. Which, yeah, I know they were exes, but I don't think he stopped caring for her. He never said a bad word about her. Not like Amber. She was the other woman in that situation. I'm sure she saw how rich Malcolm was and did everything to have him, include pushing Gail out of the picture.

Gail is going to be the mother to Lillian that my own couldn't be for me, and I think that's what has me so worked up. She is going to be so much better off without Amber in her life.

I hear a soft knock at the door and call out for whoever it is to come in. I'm pretty sure it's Asher. He would be the only one up this time of night. He comes in and cuddles me when I have nightmares. He even sleeps with his bedroom door open so he can hear me.

When Asher's head pops around the corner, I give him a watery smile. He's wearing a dark tee and shorts, which is weird for this time of the morning. He likes to sleep in his boxers.

"I just heard you and realized it was about the baby. You have a baby sister now?" he asks as he slips into the room, leaving the door slightly ajar, as per house rules. He's not supposed to be in my room without the door open. Like they don't know what we get up to when they're not home.

I nod and wipe the tears away. He sees them but doesn't say anything. He knows what they are for and has been a shoulder to cry on when I need to just let it all out. I pull back the sheets for him to come and sleep with me. He's used to this. He stays with me until I fall asleep, then he sneaks out before our parents realize.

"Yes, she's here. Lillian Hope is her name. And she looks like me as a baby, but with dark eyes." I show him the photo and he beams.

"Look how tiny she is. So small and cute. You have the cutest baby sister, Mila. Just as cute as you." He kisses my nose, and I get butterflies.

This is how I fell in love with him. There was no way I would have been able to stop that from happening. We have been together for five months now, and it's perfect. Every little thing is perfect when it comes to my guys. Summer break is coming up, and I can't wait to spend every day with them all.

"I love you, Asher."

He pulls me down under the covers and wraps his hands around me. I nestle my face into his chest and swing my leg over his. "I love you, Mila." He kisses my forehead. "Now, get some sleep before I have to sneak out."

I smile sleepily into his chest and breathe him in. I love the way he smells.

I wake to someone clearing his throat. And it's not Asher, who tenses beside me, making me realize he's still in my room and the room is light. It's morning and we slept in. Oh, crap.

"I didn't sneak out, did I?" he whispers loudly for everyone to hear, and my dad grunts.

"You two know the rules, and I don't want to ground you both," Kate says, but she's not mad.

I smile, remembering what she told Gail about me. But I don't want her to be upset. We only slept. We didn't do anything else. But I don't know how grounding us is going to help the situation... Just means we will spend more time together.

I quickly throw the blankets off. "As you can see, we're clothed."

Asher grabs me and flips me so I'm against his body, and I feel his erection poking my ass. *Oh shit.* My eyes widen. *Morning wood.*

I bite my lip to stop myself from laughing. Kate and Dad stare at us, and then Madison walks in and Asher groans from behind me. This is kinda funny. I wiggle just a little to look like I'm trying to get away. Only, I'm rubbing my ass on his cock. He holds me still and snorts.

"I'm sorry," I say. "I had a surprise call last night, and it was... emotional and Asher heard me crying and came in and we just slept. That's it. We left the door open. I promise."

Kate's expression changes from disappointed to worried in a split second. "What phone call?" she asks, and my dad comes to sit on the side of the bed, and Asher still won't let me go.

I wanna laugh so bad that I put him in an awkward position by getting rid of the blankets. I just wanted them to know we are clothed under here. No naughty business... well, apart from the dream Asher must have been having before we were woken up.

"Mom... Amber. She had the baby. Gail called to tell me and, together, we named her."

Kate sits on the other side of Asher, and he buries his face in my hair, which has fallen out from the topknot it was in last night. I hear him mumble something, and all I make out is, "Just kill me now." This is a king-size bed, but all of a sudden it feels really small.

"That's such a beautiful thing to do, Mila," Kate

says. "What did you name her?"

I smile. "Lillian Hope."

"Congratulations, big sister." My dad kisses my head, and I reach up to hug him, but Asher doesn't let go of my waist.

"Asher, let go of her. You can have her later," Madison says as she jumps up on the bed and tries to hug me around Asher. But Asher won't move from me. His dick is glued to me.

"Asher, will you just let go of Mila," Kate says, and then Dad looks over at Asher and must realize what's going on.

"Ahh… you two get up and ready for the day. I'm going to make pancakes to celebrate." He then rounds up Kate and Madison, and they close the door behind them.

I roll over and so does Asher. With his hands on his face, he groans but doesn't say anything.

"Man, that wasn't embarrassing or anything," I tease him, and the corner of his mouth tilts up in a smile. I poke his side and he groans again.

"Ugh… I can't have pancakes now. How will your dad ever look at me again?"

I pull one of his hands away and he lets me, opening one eye and looking up at me. He's so cute. I kiss him on the cheek, and he rolls his eye at me. I giggle.

"That's what you do to me, Mila. And now your dad—*my coach*—just saw me holding on to you to hide my morning wood. And you didn't help at all, wiggling that sexy ass of yours all over me."

I look down and see how bad it really is, and he catches me looking at his cock through his shorts. My eyes widen at the sight. "I didn't realize you don't have boxers on. You're naked under your shorts, and that's really... out there." I point to the massive tent in his basketball shorts. They are so loose, you can really see how hard he is.

"Yes, and you can see why the sudden sheet removal was bad... so much worse than I could have imagined."

I tickle his side, and he bends toward me. "Stop it." He playfully shoves me away. I smirk and tickle him again.

"Okay, you asked for it." He jumps on the bed, and his eyes sparkle as he jumps down on me, lifting his weight from my body before landing on me. I can feel him... all over. He starts to tickle me. I laugh and he does too.

"I can't go and have breakfast and look your dad in the eye. He knows I get excited around you now. And that's so fucking weird."

"Okay, I have a secret, but you can't tell anyone. I promise it's way worse than my dad knowing you had morning wood."

His eyes sparkle as he nods, and I chuckle. "Well, I had this teddy bear called Bedtime Bear..."

Jace is never gonna find out.

CHAPTER 19
ASHER

Jace walks in, only wearing his boxers, while I'm making coffee in Hunter's kitchen. I give him a nod good morning, but I really need my coffee to function today. I'll take one up for her, then come back and have one myself.

Mila kept us up late last night, and I'm exhausted. And not in the usual keeping-us-up-late way. She has her period and wants comfort food and movies. She made us watch *The Twilight Saga*... all four movies. I have no idea how, with four guys and one girl, we end up watching so many chick flicks. And yes, I have seen the Twilight movies before with Madison. But I was hoping for something with action, not a romance with a vampire who sparkles.

Jace smacks the back of my arm to get me to move out of his way, and I turn to him. "You a caveman?

You could have just asked me to move." Then, I smack him back. *Fucker.*

He smacks me again, and I glare at him. I move away with Mila's coffee and then quickly smack the back of his head. He turns to me, and I smile. He's not going to get the last word here... well, last smack. I walk away with Mila's coffee, and that's when he smacks my head, and the coffee sloshes over the edge of the mug and onto the tiles.

"Enough." I step back and place the mug on the counter before getting a cloth to clean up the mess he made. I look over at him. His back is turned as he makes himself coffee.

I wipe up the spill, and before I put the cloth in the sink, I wind it up and smack him on the ass with it. He jumps and calls out, and I snicker. He turns and I swear he's going to hit me. I tilt my chin, daring him, but he backs down when we hear Mila's sweet voice.

She pauses when she sees us. Her eyes narrow like she isn't sure what she just walked into. "What are you guys doing?"

I pass her the coffee and point at Jace. "He started it."

His brows rise, and Jace shakes his head and points at me.

I quickly shake my head. "Oh, hell no. You can't blame me. You came in and smacked me."

"You whipped my ass with the cloth, and that

hurt, fucker." Jace pouts at Mila, trying to get sympathy.

Ugh… what the fuck, man?

Mila's head ping-pongs between the two of us. Then Jace reaches out and smacks my arm, again. I growl and smack him back. He grabs me in a head-lock and smacks my forehead.

"Fuck off." I twist out of his arm and whack him on the head.

All the while, Mila just watches us and drinks her coffee. Hunter emerges and makes a coffee around Jace and me.

"This is the last one, okay?" I'm red from where he's struck me. They aren't hard hits, but they sting like a bitch. "Just one more—that's it," I tell him. I hold my hand up and he does the same.

"One, two, three, go," I count.

We both smack each other's shoulders, then he gives me an extra smack.

I grit my teeth. "That was two, asshole," I grumble and he shakes his head.

"That's for the one earlier."

I throw my hands up. "What one earlier? I swear to god, no more. I'm done."

He smacks my head when I turn my back on him, and I launch at him, wrestling him to the ground. "What the hell is your problem?" I yell at him, tapping his forehead as he's pinned to the floor.

"I could ask the same." He flips me and smacks

me on my ribs. It fucking stings, and I cry out at him to stop.

"Is someone going to stop this?" Mila asks from where she's perched on a stool, looking over the counter at us, and I wonder the same.

"Stop, you two," Hunter says sarcastically.

I roll my eyes. "Stop it, Jace. It's done," I tell him, and he lets up. We're both sitting there in our boxers, breathing heavily.

"If you two want to fuck each other, can you do it somewhere else? We're trying to have coffee," Hunter jokes, and I laugh.

Jace shoves me, and I don't care. *Whatever*. I throw my hands up and get up. Is that what this was about? Is he weirded out over me and Hunter kissing? He wasn't even there for that, and we haven't sat around talking about it. It hasn't happened since that night... but I hope it does. I want to kiss Hunter again.

"I don't want to fuck anyone but Mila," Jace growls.

I don't know why, but I laugh, because he hasn't even done that.

"Stop fighting." Mila stands, holding her hands up for us to stop. I don't move. I stand where I am and wait to see what Jace does.

"Sorry," he mumbles, but I have no idea why he even started this.

I nod.

"Say you're sorry," Mila says to me.

I don't need to say sorry. This is bullshit. Jace started it.

"Sorry," I mutter to Jace, not meaning it at all. I eye Jace, and I can see he knows it; he was only apologizing for Mila. This isn't finished.

Whatever *this* is.

It's been a week since Jace had me in a headlock at Hunter's. Mom and James are out doing wedding shopping. It's getting close—only a month away. Madison is off shopping with Bella, and it's just Mila and me here… alone.

I put some music on in the kitchen, knowing she will come in here to turn it off. I sit on the counter and wait for her.

Less than a minute later, she's in the kitchen, with bright pink socks pulled up to her knees. She's wearing my basketball shorts and an oversized hoodie that belongs to Roman. Her hair is up in that messy bun she does, and little tendrils have fallen free, and she looks absolutely beautiful. She sees me and stops. Putting her hand on her hip, she cocks her head at me.

I chuckle and turn the music off.

"Why do you torture me, Asher? How can you listen to that crap?"

I jump off the counter and stalk over to her. She doesn't move, and when we're toe to toe, she looks up at me and I smile down at her.

Fuck, she is gorgeous. I can't believe I can just kiss her, and she will kiss me back. Every day, I count myself lucky that she's mine.

The thing between us—the butterflies, as she calls them—haven't changed at all. They're still there every day, and I hope they stay around for the rest of our lives. This girl came into my world and shook everything up.

I never wanted a girlfriend. And I definitely never wanted one who already had boyfriends I'd have to share her with. I'd always pictured going to college and fucking random chicks on the weekends. Never settling down, never finding love.

Then Mila fucking Hart happened.

"You are the most gorgeous girl in the entire world. And would you like to join me in the hot tub... *naked*?"

She giggles and chews on her bottom lip. I reach down and pull it from her teeth, and she smiles up at me. "Mmm, is there an orgasm involved?"

I chuckle. "For you? Always."

She pretends to think, and I can't wait out the game any longer. Reaching down, I wrap my arms around her thighs and lift her. She squeals and holds onto my shoulders to steady herself. She wraps her legs around my waist, and I pull her down, so our faces are together.

"Well, okay then, bossy boots. I will have my orgasm in the spa and a back massage." She rubs her body against me while I kiss her.

I smack her ass. "Which one first?" Does she want a back rub first? Or for me to make her come first? I can probably think of a way to make both those things happen at the same time.

"Come first, then massage."

She has been up in her room, drawing and sketching every day. She's probably hurt her back from staying in the same position for too long.

I'm just grateful it's summer, school is out, and Mila is my girl.

I drop her beside the hot tub and remove the hoodie. As she stands, topless, I drop the hoodie on the ground. She doesn't even have a bra on. Fuck, she has the nicest tits. Did she know I was going to suggest the hot tub?

She laughs. "Stop staring at me. These are called boobs." She waves at them, and I roll my eyes and laugh.

"Yes, normally they are contained in a bra, so I was surprised. Sorry, but I'm a guy. I'm gonna stare at your boobs if you're gonna show them off."

She swats me away when I reach for one. "Hey, no touching the goods until I see what you're packing for me."

She doesn't have to tell me twice to take off my shorts. I strip in record time. "What do you think?" I wave my hand over my body and wiggle a little to show her the goods.

Mila giggles. "Are you always excited to see me... or was it the boobs?"

I reach for her and wrap my arms around her, swinging her around as I kiss her. "Boobs."

She shakes her head but grins up at me. "Boobs. You're such a guy."

I shrug. What can I say? I like boobs. I grab her ass in my hand, and she squeaks. "And asses." Then, I give it a little smack and she jumps. I pull her up into my arms as I climb into the spa and lower her between my legs.

"Mmm... I needed this. God, this is perfect." She rolls her neck around, and I massage her, rubbing my thumbs into her knots.

"You need better posture while you're working."

Mila turns and kisses me. Her tongue meets mine, and I moan, forgetting about the massage. My hands travel to her breasts, and her body presses into me as I rub my thumbs over her nipples. My cock is hard as I rub it against her ass.

She spins and straddles me. Looking down into my eyes, she bites her lip. "I'm gonna fuck you so good, Asher, you're not gonna remember your name."

I love when she's wild and free like this.

"My name's Asher, so you better get to work. All talk and no action." I slap her ass in the water, and she bucks into my cock.

She trails her hands down my chest, her fingertips running over my abs until she reaches my cock. I hiss at the touch... God, her hand is so tiny wrapped around my cock. Makes me look huge. She strokes me, and I moan, my head dropping back on the edge of the hot tub.

"That feels so good, Mila. Fuck, you always feel so good."

I can feel her pussy grinding against me too, and I grip her hips and rub her against my length. She moans as I hit her clit over and over. I suck her nipple into my mouth, and she arches her back as I nip and suck.

"Oh fuck, keep doing that. I'm close."

I know those magic words... they literally mean keep doing what I'm doing. Don't stop, don't change speed, and keep the same pressure. Her body breaks out into goose bumps. The warm water and cool air of the day mix with the pleasure.

"Come for me, Mila." I suck her other nipple into my mouth, and she gasps, her body stilling as she shudders. I hold her tight as I reach down and rub her clit.

"Asher," she whimpers as she collapses on my chest.

After a few aftershocks, I let up on her, rubbing circles along her back and kissing her head.

She draws back and kisses me. Wrapping her arms around my neck, she raises herself up over me. Pulling back, she looks down to where I'm stroking my cock against her.

She moves a little closer, and I notch myself at her entrance. She lowers herself, and we both groan. Fuck, she's so perfect. She takes my lips again, and I hold her ass as she slowly fucks herself against my cock. I want to take over, go harder and deeper, but I let Mila set the pace for now.

She moans, throwing her head back and riding me. God, I wish I could take a photo and show her how pretty she looks riding me.

"Fuck me," she whispers into my ear, and I do.

My hips piston up, and I slam into her over and over. She moans loudly, and I worry the neighbors might hear that, so I slow down, rotate my hips, and rock against her clit over and over until she gasps, and I can't hold back.

"I'm. Gonna. Come," I barely get out as my abs tighten and I thrust one last time. With a deep groan, I come deep inside her and shudder as she clenches around my cock and comes. We're both breathing heavily, and she collapses on my chest. I hug her tight to my chest and lower us deeper into the water.

"Oh shit, that was so good. We need to come out here more when the parents aren't around."

She giggles. "Water and sex don't mix that well… Now I'm worried to get off your dick, because what went up must come down, and I don't want your cum floating in the hot tub. That's gross."

Well, when she says it like that, it's gross. I didn't think about that. I just got excited to spend some one-on-one time with her.

I lift her and stand, my cock still buried deep inside her. Walking us to the towels, I grab one, trying to hold her to me and not let go. I wrap it around her shoulders and walk toward the house. Only, my dick isn't as hard now, and it slips out, and I can feel the tickle of my cum run down my balls.

I stop. Well, that's the weirdest feeling, ever.

CHAPTER 20
MILA

t's not every day your dad gets married to his soulmate. But today's the day, and Kate's freaking out. Not in an *I can't marry him* way. But in a *what if this is a disaster* way. It won't be a disaster. It's a perfect, small, backyard wedding at the house, and it looks amazing. We've spent the last two days decorating. Roman, Jace, and Hunter helped us all out since there was so much to do.

"Do you have water, girls?" Kate asks. "It might get hot out there."

I nod. I hold up the water bottle she gave me and put it in the little bag that matches my dress. Madison shows her too. We're wearing matching red satin dresses, and Kate is wearing a cream one with the most beautiful lace bodice. She looks like a princess. She doesn't look older than my dad... She's not much older, but she doesn't look her age.

Kate pauses with her hand out like she's about to say something else and turns to her mother. "Do you think the wedding cake is too much?"

"No, I think it's the most amazing cake you have ever made, dear."

"It's too much, too big for how many guests we have. Do we have enough seats? Did we get too many?" Kate starts again, and I don't know what to do or say.

I look at Madison, and her eyes widen, like we are having a secret conversation. I roll my eyes and shrug. I have no idea what's going on with Kate. Is this what happens at a wedding—you stress over everything? Doesn't seem like the most magical day of your life when you're so anxious.

"Is that the song? The one we're supposed to come out to?" Madison asks me, shuffling forward to see everyone out there ready to go.

Kate hears her and flies into a panic. Shit, she's not ready yet. She needs to collect herself.

I have seen cool and calm Kate. I have seen loving and caring Kate and disappointed Kate... And now I can add crazy Kate to the list. Oh my god. I don't know what to do, but now she's bent over, hyperventilating, her hair is a mess, and even Madison has no idea what to do. We're just standing still and watching this weird scene unfold.

"Can one of you girls go tell them to start the

song again?" Kate's mom asks. "Your mother is having a moment."

My heart swells at the way she said "your mother." It's only Madison and me in here with Grandma —as she insisted I call her—and Kate.

Well, if that doesn't pull heart strings.

"I'll go do it, Grandma." It feels weird to say it at first, but she smiles at me. I've never had real grandparents. Not like this, anyway. And I love her already and hope I can keep her forever.

"Good girl, Mila." She nods, and the words bring other thoughts to mind.

Jace has ruined those words for me. But we still haven't had sex. We do everything but sex. He is waiting. And I love his patience, but I don't know what he's waiting for. But man, when he gives in and takes me… that's going to be an epic night. I swear, he's getting me back for all the times I teased him.

I rush out of the house and wave at Hunter. He's controlling the music for the wedding. It's a great turnout of family and friends. Asher is Dad's best man, and he looks so handsome in his tux. I bet he's hot out there in the sun. The weather brought out the best day of the year and is trying to fry us all under the sun.

Hunter looks over at me, and his mouth drops open. Oh shit. I forgot the guys haven't seen me yet. I wave for him to stop the song and wait to do it again.

Well, I hope he understood my hand gestures. He nods.

That's when I see that everyone's staring at me. Now I'm feeling nervous. I'm not one for attention. I put on a smile and back up to the house and slip into the door. Kate's standing there, red roses in her hands, and she looks all put together. Like she wasn't in here having a nervous breakdown only moments before.

"Okay, we are ready, girls. Mila, you're first. Once you step out there, tell that handsome fella of yours to start the music."

I grin. Grandma has taken a liking to Hunter. But who wouldn't? He's very easy on the eyes, and he can charm the pants off anyone. And he did that to Grandma already.

I walk outside, and everyone turns to see me again. Only, this time, I nod to Hunter, and he starts the song again. Elvis rings out, and everyone turns and looks at me. Well, okay. I didn't expect so many eyes on me. I realize then I forgot my flowers. *Shit.*

"Mila," Madison says from behind me.

Turning, I see she's holding my white roses, and I quickly take them and whisper, "Thank you."

I walk slowly down the aisle. Everyone's watching, and when Madison and I get to the end, we turn to watch Kate walking down the aisle. I look at my dad, and he brings out a tissue and dabs his eyes. I haven't seen my dad cry many times and watching him as his future wife and soulmate walks down the aisle to him chokes me up.

I sniffle and try not to look. But then I see Asher's eyes welling up, and that's it. Why the hell don't I have a tissue in my little bag? I don't need water... my mascara is running, and I didn't expect to experience so many emotions.

Jace sneaks up and hands me a tissue. He looks at Madison, who's crying too, and hands her one before returning to his seat beside Daniel and Ella. Jace came prepared. Who would have known?

When Kate makes her way to Dad, I hear him whisper, "You are the most beautiful woman in the world." Thankfully, Kate came prepared and pulls out a tissue of her own. I already need another tissue. That's so sweet. My dad's a romantic.

Everyone sits down and the ceremony begins.

I'm buzzed. I had a few too many glasses of champagne, and now I'm lying on Roman in the family room, and the room is spinning.

"Mila, babe, you need some water." Hunter hands me a water, and I swat it away.

Roman growls and takes it from him. "Drink," he grunts.

I giggle and tap him on the nose. "Boop, Mr.

Bossy. You drink the water. I need to dance." I try to wiggle my way off his lap, but he holds me tighter. I stop and pout up at him, but Roman doesn't fall for my tricks, ever. His eyes penetrate mine, and I sigh.

"Fine, I'll drink. Then, *Mr. Bossy pants I don't dance*, you'll come dance."

He shakes his head as he opens the bottle and puts it to my lips. I roll my eyes, but I take a sip of the cool water. Then I take the bottle from him and drink more. Okay, I needed the water. I dribble a little down my chin and onto my dress. I giggle, but then, when I look down at my dress and see the satin is a mess, I feel terrible that I ruined my dress.

As the day grew into the night, I had fun dancing and drinking with Madison. Jace and Hunter danced with me. Roman watched me from the sidelines. Asher danced with me awkwardly. Apparently, it's okay that I'm dating three guys, but I'm not allowed to show the family that I'm also with Asher. I agreed to that, because I would rather Kate not get questions about it on her special day.

I know our relationship isn't conventional, and I hate how people judge us. But I don't want that for Dad and Kate on their wedding day. Plus, everyone just saw them get married, and Asher became my stepbrother officially.

I grin. "Oh, stepbrother, please help me. I wanna dance."

Asher's hands go to his face, and he mutters

something, and I giggle. He hates this, and I find it so funny.

"It's a little funny," I call out to him. It's the reason we kept each other at arm's length as long as we did —in case this day happened. And it just did.

"Yeah, Asher. Go dance with your new sister," Jace teases, and Asher shoves him.

I sigh. I don't want another repeat of them hitting each other. It's like a play fight that just goes too far. I honestly don't get it. But they seem cool with each other most the time.

I wave my fingers at Asher, and he playfully rolls his eyes at me as he stands. He won't deny me a dance. He takes my hand and slowly extracts me from Roman.

Asher wraps his arm around me and holds me close. My head rests against his chest and he sways me. We can be close here. It's just the guys and Madison, who has fallen asleep, curled in a ball on the armchair. I point to her and Jace nods at me. I watch as he gets a blanket from the back of the couch and drapes that over her and tucks it in.

He's so sweet. I look at Hunter, who's sitting beside Roman, and they're talking and laughing. Both have a smile on their face, and I look up to Asher.

He pushes some hair behind my ear and gives me a small smile. "I love you." He chuckles a little before kissing me.

"I love you too." I sigh and hold him close.

So glad that I took a chance on love... and won the lottery.

CHAPTER 21
HUNTER

can't believe I'm going to see my mom today. She's been away for so long, but Dad's driving her back today. I haven't seen him in over a month. He called me yesterday to tell me he was bringing her home and to have lunch prepared.

"Do you think we made enough?" Roman asks, pacing the kitchen.

Since he never returned to school after he came back from New York City with Mila, he took up the role of homemaker. He cooks and cleans, and he's good at it.

"Sandwiches? There's enough to feed us for a week. I think you need to stop in the kitchen. Come take a seat." I tap the chair beside me.

He hesitates at first then puts down the cloth he'd been cleaning with. His hair is pulled back into a bun, and he smooths it with his hands. He fiddles with the edge of his shirt… Yes, he's wearing a shirt with buttons. Looks good on him. But I won't tell him that. He's worked up right now. He's acting more nervous than me, and I don't know why.

"Kate is baking Mom a red velvet cake. It's her favorite, and they will all be over this afternoon. So, I think you just need to relax. My parents will be here any minute."

Hearing the front door, I stand, pull down my tee, and hold the back of the chair. When I see my mom round the corner, I run to her, my throat thick with emotion as I take her in.

"Hunter, baby." She holds her arms wide, and I bend down, wrapping my arms around her.

"Mom," I choke out. "I missed you so much." Fuck, I didn't think I would cry. Mom's home and she looks amazing.

I pull back and look down at her. Her big, dark eyes, the same as mine, are bright and demon free. Her hair's different. I tug on the ends, and she reaches up.

"I had it cut. I think it suits me."

I nod. It does. She looks like a totally different person. I wish this had happened years ago. I would have loved to see her like this and not the person she used to be.

"I think it looks lovely, Angela," Roman says, and she opens her arms to him and he goes over and hugs her. She looks so tiny in Roman's arms.

"Dad," I go to him and shake his hand. He nods.

Roman nods at him but doesn't make a move toward him. It's suddenly awkward in here, and I think my dad just gives off a vibe whenever he's around Roman. I know he never liked our friendship. I'm at Lakeview now, so he can't complain about me not doing what he wants. This was the deal. Lakeview for Roman.

"Let's eat," I suggest. "Roman made lunch for us all."

Mom hums and walks over to the table to inspect everything. Roman really outdid himself with the spread. He remembered Mom likes those little sandwiches and made so many.

"Oh, Roman. This looks wonderful." Then she gasps. "Oh, wow. These are my favorite." She turns to Roman, and he blushes under her praise, looking anywhere but at Mom.

"He remembered and made them for you." She puts her hand to her chest, and I can tell she's gonna cry, so I quickly distract her. "Here, Mom. Take a seat and we can all eat them."

I gesture to Dad to come sit too, but he lingers near the door. I don't get him. I haven't seen him or heard from him in a month, and he won't even come and sit down to have a meal with us.

Roman can sense the tension and sits beside Mom. They both take plates and start filling them up with those fancy sandwiches.

Dad waves for me to come over and then walks out the room. Shit. I look back at Mom. She has the back of her head to me, and Roman glances past her. I don't want to leave Mom. She only just got home, but Roman sees and nods, putting his arm around her chair in a protective gesture, and I relax a little. I had no idea I was so worked up. She's home now. She won't be leaving me again.

"Roman. You sure know how to spoil a lady," Mom mumbles around a mouthful, and he smiles.

I take a deep breath and find my dad. He's down in the living room; it's all cleaned up after our sleep-over the night before. It's become a habit of ours, but now that Mom's back, no fun times at the sleep-overs... at least, out here. We'll have to move playtime to the bedroom. I don't want my mom walking into that. I don't think I could look her in the eye again if she caught what goes on down here.

Dad stands in the room, his back to me, looking at the family photo we had taken when I was seven. The three of us are all smiling like a happy family, but you can see the cracks even there.

"Hunter, I wanted to come tell you today in person that I have asked your mother for a divorce."

I grit my teeth, but I've known this was coming. It's something I wished for long ago when they would spend all their free time fighting.

"Mom just got home. Couldn't you have waited a few days?" He could have at least given my mother back before she spirals and starts drinking again. I'm going to have to make sure that doesn't happen. With Roman here, we can take care of her. She'll be fine. I stretch my fingers out, trying to avoid hitting something.

"I asked her before she went into rehab. I wanted to do one last thing for you before I made it official. Your mother was in a bad place, and now she's back and will be stable for you."

I shake my head. I don't get this. "Why didn't you do this years ago? Why now? You never told me you were taking her. She was just gone. You just took her and wouldn't let me speak to her for months. I've been here alone for months, and you have spoken to me less than a handful of times. You didn't even come home for Christmas."

I can't stop the anger leaking from me. This is total bullshit. But good riddance.

He shakes his head. "I met someone, and we're getting married."

I have nothing to say to him. I turn my back and walk out when he calls out,

"I'm selling the house. Your mother will get half. That's fair enough. But the house will be on the market by the end of the week."

"That's fair enough?" I scream out. "Really? Fair to who? The woman who did everything to get you through college, start your career while she stayed home and watched you fucking people behind her back? That's fair? Half a house. Well, fuck you. Get out." I launch at him and shove him backward, and he hits the wall. The family photo of our three fake-smiling faces falls and the glass shatters.

I see the seven-year-old staring back at me, and my breath catches.

"Mom, do you think Daddy will like me wearing my blue shirt?" I smile up at her as I do the last button. She pulls on one of my curls and it bounces back up. I giggle when she sticks her tongue out.

"Yes, he will wear a blue shirt too. You will look like twins." I giggle. I don't look like my dad. I look more like my mommy, I think. We have the same darker skin, whereas daddy doesn't have that.

Mommy undoes all the buttons for me and straightens them up. I never get them all in the right holes. But she doesn't care; she just helps me without telling me off. Not like Daddy. He gets mad and yells at me if I get them wrong. I don't like shirts. They make me itchy.

"Hurry, or we will be late," Dad calls from the living room.

I run down the stairs and smile up at him. I straighten out my shirt, and he looks down at me and frowns.

"That shirt looks too big on you. Go change."

I look down at the shirt Mommy bought me only yesterday, and my shoulders sag. I don't have another blue shirt. This is the only one.

"We only got that yesterday, Thomas. It was for the photos today. I thought it would be nice if we're all in blue. Like a family."

I turn to Mom and see she's distressed. I can feel when Mom is sad, and I hate that I can't always make it better. "I think you look really pretty, Mommy."

Daddy just snorts and shakes his head. "This photo will be on my desk for all to see. I want to look like I can afford to buy my only child clothes that fit. Go put on the red shirt that fits you, Hunter."

My heart sinks. Daddy doesn't want to be twins with me. I turn and run out of the room before he sees me cry. "Boys don't cry," he told me when he brought out his belt once to teach me what I should cry about.

I quickly change and return. My mom is staring out the window into the backyard. I don't like when she does that. It scares me sometimes. Like she's going to leave me. Not physically, but she gets lost in her head. That's what she tells me she's doing.

"I'm back," I announce with a big smile on my face, hoping everyone will be happy now.

Mom turns. Her eyes are red. I can tell she was crying while I was gone. Why does Daddy make her cry? I should have worn the red shirt. Daddy wouldn't have been upset if I wore the red one. He wouldn't have made Mommy cry.

"Get in the car. We're late now. And get yourself together, woman. We're having our family portrait taken. We are going to look like a happy family and all smile big."

He looks right at me. I swallow the lump in my throat and nod.

I take Mom's hand and we walk to the car. I give her hand an extra squeeze before I let go.

She smiles at me. "You look much better in red."

I smile. I don't want to wear blue. Blue is Daddy's color. Red is for me.

I see red. I have nothing more to say to him. A large hand lands on my shoulder. I tense, but then I hear Roman grunt, "Get out." His voice is deep and laced with warning.

My father is no match for Roman. He has never spoken to him like this before. Hell, Roman's maybe said three words, if that, to my father. And now he's telling him to leave... his own house.

I stand taller. "You heard him. Get out. You're not welcome here anymore. And I'm not going back to Lakeview. You can fuck off if you think I'm going to do what you want anymore."

Dad throws his hands up. "I'm done with trying to stop you throwing away your future. Do whatever you want. You're no son of mine anymore."

I grin. "You were never a father."

He says nothing. He just walks around the broken glass, and I see Mom standing there, tears running down her face.

"Mom," I choke out. "I'm so sorry."

She shakes her head, and I rush to her, wrapping my arms around her. "No, Hunter. I'm sorry I didn't leave him earlier."

I shake my head. That man had a hold on Mom in a way I will never understand, but she never has to apologize for it. She did what she had to, fought her demons, and got a little lost along the way. But now she's back, she's my mom, she's strong and amazing, and I love her. That's all that matters to me.

"Don't be sorry, Mom. We're better off now." I look over to Roman, who's looking down at the shattered glass, giving us this moment. But he shouldn't be.

"The three of us will be a real family now," she says.

Roman looks up, and Mom waves him over.

"Come here, Roman," she calls to him, and the big guy looks so awkward, like he doesn't know what to do.

But he finally comes over, his hands in his pockets. Mom doesn't care. She wraps her arm around him, and he shuffles in beside me. I wrap my arm over his shoulder.

"You're my boys and, together, we are a family."

CHAPTER 22
MILA

I can't believe the end of summer is already here. Senior year starts next week, and it was only a year ago I moved back here. So much has happened in one year.

I look up at the clouds and sigh as Hunter runs his hands through my hair. We're out on the grass in Hunter's backyard. Asher and Jace are messing around in the pool. Jace has Asher in a headlock; this is the new normal for them. They act like brothers, I have figured out. It's not that Jace is upset with him or anything. I think it's because Asher came in so late, and this is just the way guys bond.

At least, I hope this is it. Grady and Jace are like this too, so I'm hoping that's all. I'm also hoping they grow out of it, because I swear, the two of them drive me nuts when they're in a mood.

"Did you want any more watermelon?" Angela

hollers from the side door. Divorce and rehab look so good on her.

"No, thank you," I call out, waving at her.

Roman gets up from where he's been reading a book and jogs over to her. I watch him as he goes and bite my lip at those legs. Fuck, I want to climb him like a tree.

Sudden pleasure comes over my nipples, and I can feel it all the way down to my core. I look down, and Hunter's fingers are there, rubbing over my tee. "Hunter?"

"Just helping you out for when he comes back."

I slap his hand away. "I'm a little sore from last night, so I need some time to recover."

Hunter chuckles. Last night was fun. I wish Jace would join in, but he always makes up for it after. Asher and Hunter kissed again last night and, fuck, it was hot. Roman fucked me from behind so I could watch... I came. Hard.

They have only kissed a few times. It's like the heat of the moment, and they finally let loose a little. I want them to drop their masks and both just feel it. Be in the moment. But they can't until they're ready.

"There are people coming to look at the house later. I fucking hate that he's selling it. I wish I had the money to keep it. Did you know he pulled my college fund? He used it for a down payment on a house with his new wife. So, now college is out of the picture unless I get a bunch of student loans. I didn't need a scholarship before, but now I do. This year, I have to play hard.

"We need Roman on the team. Without him, we're gonna be shit. But I don't know how to get him back to school. He's been working at the shop with Ronnie. Even talked about buying the shop from him. I know that's what he wants, but I just want us all together. One last year."

He kisses my forehead as I watch Roman return with a plate of watermelon. Jace jumps out of the pool, dripping wet, and shakes his hair... like a dog. I giggle as Roman gets soaked. Roman shoves Jace back into the pool, and Asher gets him in a choke hold. I roll my eyes, and Roman sees it.

He grins. "Do we have to take the *children* to the party later?" he asks.

I laugh. It's so true. They're children... but I love it. It means they feel safe enough to be like this. And that's all that matters to me.

"It's Grady's going-away-to-college party," I tell him. Roman shrugs, and I giggle.

He sits down and looks back over at the two of them wrestling under the water, and I reach over and steal the watermelon from his hand. I take a big bite before he can get it back.

"Hey, you said you didn't want any."

I chew with my mouth open, and he launches himself at me, pinning me to the grass. I laugh, almost choking on the watermelon.

"That's mine. You need to give it back."

I quickly swallow and poke my tongue out at him. He growls, pinning me with my hands above my head and grinding himself into me.

I raise a brow at him. He wants to play this game? *It's on.* I wrap my legs around his waist and pull him tight and rock against him. I can feel him growing harder.

He growls into my ear. "If Angela wasn't home, I would fuck you right here on the grass where anyone could see. I would eat your pussy until you're screaming my name."

I gasp. Okay, I hadn't been expecting him to say *that*. And now I want it. Angela can just stay inside for a little longer. He pulls away, and I'm left lying there, my heart racing. The loss of pressure against my clit has me pouting. God, he's just as bad as Hunter. I swear, the two of them must sit around when I'm not here and practice dirty lines to get me all worked up.

I get up and brush myself off before looking over at the house. It's beautiful. I have always thought so. It's a big house. Big enough for all of us. There are plenty of bedrooms, enough for one each. I look at the bushes, where we wanted the treehouse to go. Fuck Hunter's dad for denying us that one little thing. He was an asshole then, and nothing has changed.

I can't believe he's selling this place. I hate that for

Hunter. It's bullshit. This place was one of my favorite places to come to growing up. Escaping in Hunter's large yard. Playing princesses and knights. Swimming in the pool. Playing football... so much football.

I smile at the memories we've made here. So many.

"Go long, Jace," Hunter says as he holds the football.

I grin. I'm gonna get him. Hunter is a terrible quarterback, yelling out his calls for everyone to hear. Roman looks at me and nods. We're ready for them.

As soon as Jace runs, I barrel toward Hunter and tackle him before the ball even leaves his hand.

"Mila, ugh, get off me." He groans under me.

I stand up and hold out my hand to pull him up. He takes it and shoots to his feet, his curls bobbing on his head, and I smile. I love his curls; they are so cute. He hates when I tell him that, so I try not to. I pull on one, and he swats my hand away.

"Mila. You promised you would give me five seconds."

I purse my lips. I did. "Sorry, I just got excited." I can't help it. This is why Dad says I can't play defense anymore. I tend to tackle first and think later. I like to win, especially against the boys.

Roman runs to me and high-fives me. He's wearing a huge smile, and his hair is flopping over his face. He pushes it behind his ear and looks me up and down.

"That was hard, Mila. Are you okay?"

I dust the dirt off my knee. "Nah, I don't hurt. Hunter?" I turn to see him limping away. My heart squeezes in my chest. I hurt him. I didn't mean to. Dad was right. I need to stop being on defense. I can't hurt my friends. Especially Hunter. He's the smallest of us all, so I have to be gentler.

I follow him to our secret spot. "Are you okay?" I ask. When he turns to me, he shakes his head, and I can see tears on his cheeks. "Oh no, Hunter, I'm so sorry. I'll get your mom."

He reaches out and takes my hand. It's warm in mine, and I hold him back. He looks down at our hands and shakes his head. "No, don't. She's sleeping. I'm not hurt. Not really." He lets go of my hand and looks up at me, those big chocolate eyes of his filled with tears, and mine do the same.

I quickly sit next to him. "It's okay. I will fix you. I can get some ice and make you feel better." I try to stand again, but he holds my arm tight.

"I'm not crying from my ankle. It's just… everything. Dad. Just… don't leave. Stay here with me?"

I nod on his shoulder as he holds me and cries. I cry with him; my mom and dad fight too, and it makes me cry. So, I know how it feels to keep it in all day.

I wish we had our treehouse here. It's so pretty, and the trees would hide it from everyone. Maybe we can build one, and Hunter's dad can't say no, then. It will be our secret, like our secret spot.

. . .

Holy shit. I know how to keep Hunter's house. I'm not going to college—I don't need money for that—but Gail said college and a first home.

I look up at the house again. It's huge... It's not a first house a normal person buys. But I know how much is in that bank account, and I have more than enough to buy it. Why didn't I think of this sooner?

I scramble to my feet and look for my cell.

Hunter peers up at me. "Did you lose something?"

I nod. "My cell." He reaches behind him and hands it to me.

"Thanks." I rush off barefoot to the secret spot and find Joe's number. I haven't spoken to him since... well, since then. I wonder if he will even remember me. After pressing dial, I put the cell to my ear. I pace, pulling on the ends of my hair as I wait.

"Mila Hart, how may I help you?" Joe says, and I smile.

"I want to buy a house..."

CHAPTER 23
MILA

I take a sip of my beer and wave to Grady. He raises his beer to me, and I smile. It's good to be back at a party. I feel like it's been forever since the last one.

"Hey, Mila." Emerson smiles wildly at me. "You miss me?"

"Fuck, Em. Yes, I missed you." I jump up and launch myself at him as I wrap my arms around his neck and pull him in for the biggest hug. Since I haven't been back at school and have pretty much become a hermit, just staying home or going wherever the guys go, I haven't seen him in so long.

"Don't hug me too tight. Your boyfriends might get jealous and come hurt me," he teases, then slaps my ass.

I chuckle. He's just looking for trouble now.

"You're a big, tough boy now, Em. You can fight them all off."

He grins and shakes his head at me. "That was before. Now they're more protective of you than you realize. And there's no way I want to get in between you and them."

I laugh. *It's true*, I think as I watch Jace eyeing us. I wink at him, and he knows I'm up to no good. He doesn't tell Em off for slapping my ass, though. He knows it's all in good fun.

Emerson drops me to my feet, and I think back to the day I first came home, when I crashed their party. It feels like forever ago. "Remember when I came back, and Jace wasn't happy that I was here at his party?"

Emerson's smile widens as he nods. Fuck, Emerson's going to break hearts when he's at college. Only one more year to go. I'm going back to school for my senior year. So is Roman. He doesn't know it yet, but Joe is getting us back in. He told me he can work magic, and if he gets us back into Ridgecrest... I will believe him.

"I totally was going to take you back to my room and have my wicked way with you," I tell him. It's the truth. He's all grown up, but I had changed my ways. No more meaningless sex. So, it didn't happen. But I sure was tempted.

Emerson bursts out laughing. "That's so funny. I would have let you, too. Trust me. Growing up, I had a little crush on you. But in a scared way. Like, you might hurt me, but I'm gonna like it."

I smack his arm, and he points to where I just hit him. "See, exactly my point."

"That didn't hurt, you big baby." I push him, and he stumbles back a step. He's been drinking for a while. He's huge, so there's no way I could do that normally. He let me.

"You know I'm the better looking one, right? You can have your wicked way with me now... You're not as scary now that I'm taller than you."

I stand back and hold my chin as I pretend to check Emerson out. I feel arms wrap around my waist and hold me back from him, and I laugh.

"Don't be looking at him," Jace growls into my ear.

I love this side of him. So protective and alpha. I wake the beast inside, and I love to see how far I can push him before I'm on my knees and he's fucking my mouth, calling me a good girl. I love it. It's our dynamic.

"But I was thinking four wasn't enough."

I squeal as Jace lifts me over his shoulder and smacks my ass. I see an upside-down Emerson shaking his head as Jace walks me away from him.

"Don't be teasing me, Mila. Or I'll have to punish you."

"I know the way you like to punish me, Jace. And I've been a very bad girl."

He lets out a groan, knowing that we really shouldn't be sneaking off right now. This is Grady's going-away party. He's off to college, and I'm so proud of him. He worked really hard and had a lot of shit thrown at him this past year. But he's found an amazing college that offered him a scholarship. That's accepting of who he is as a person, and he won't be very far from us. It's only about an hour's drive, so I will see him on weekends. And go to his games.

I notice Walker has arrived late to the party. Fashionably late, as always. He's going to the same college as Grady. It's not the college I thought he would end up at. Kind of thought he had a Harvard or Yale type of family. But he's going to the same small college and playing on the football team as their quarterback.

I never asked him why he picked that college, but I have a feeling it's because of his mom. Walker might be all talk and full of flirty comebacks, but he has a heart of gold when it comes to his mom. Anybody who really knows him can see that. And it makes me love him as a friend all the more.

"Hey, sweet cheeks," Walker says to my ass.

"Shut up," Jace growls, but he doesn't really mean it.

He's come to like Walker. He gets riled up from the things Walker says, to the point I think they will hit each other, but then the next thing, they're playing Xbox and acting like best friends. It's the strangest friendship, but hey, it works.

Jace drops me to my feet and points his finger at me, but I see the gleam in his eye. "Don't check him out either. Four is more than enough, and we will soon show you that."

I wink up at him. "Is that a promise? All of you tonight?"

Jace lets out an exhausted breath and shakes his head. He looks over at Walker, who grins at me. "You two have fun, but not too much fun. I'm getting a drink."

I giggle as Jace kisses my head and leaves me with Walker.

"What's that about?" Walker asks with his brows raised.

"He doesn't wanna join in on any fun and games. I think he has performance anxiety in front of the guys." I know it's not true but more that he has sharing issues. We've talked about it.

Walker chokes on his beer, and I burst out laughing.

"Mila, you dirty minx. Well, if he's not willing to take part, I know somebody who is." He wiggles his brows at me.

I love that he doesn't give up now that I'm with them all. That he still teases me like the first day we met. I love this about Walker. He is who he is, and he's unapologetic.

I tap my beer to his, and his beer slushes over onto our feet, and I giggle again.

"Is someone a little drunk?"

I nod. Now that everything bad is behind us, and we can look forward to our future, I decided to let down my hair and get drunk tonight. It's not like I'm at a party alone; I have my four guys here to take care of me. I love the fact that they don't smother me. They let me walk around and talk to all my friends. But they still keep an eye on me. Keep me safe.

I glance at Britney, who came with one of the other seniors, and she hasn't left his side since. It's obvious he's getting annoyed that she's just always there. That would drive me nuts if the guys were like that.

"I promise not to take advantage of you, sweet cheeks, if you promise not to punch me," Walker says. "My mother would be all too happy to find out you were secretly in love with me this whole time."

I burst out laughing. "That is never gonna happen. But I would love to come over and watch movies with your mom. Is that all right with you?" I've been meaning to ask him since he got accepted. I know he won't be around as much, and I want to help him out. Even if it's just to check in on his mom so he doesn't have to worry about her as much.

Walker wraps his arm around my shoulders and pulls me in for a side hug. "That's more than all right with me, and if you are driving past my house during the week while I'm away, I'm sure she would love the company."

"Your mom is cool and has great taste in movies."

He gives me a squeeze. He won't say it. When things get deep, he shuts down. He's similar to Hunter in that way.

The music grows louder, and I look to see Hunter turning it up. His shirt is off, and all his delicious abs are on display. He dances, and that's my cue to go rub against my boyfriend's chest and claim him in front of all these girls ogling him.

I haven't felt this hungover in forever. My mouth is dry, and I groan, rolling away from a furnace. I have no idea who's sleeping beside me, but they are hot as hell. What time did we even get home last night? I shove my feet out from under the sheets. I need to cool down before I move. I think I wanna throw up.

Looking over, I see it's Hunter who is my personal heater. His face is relaxed, and he looks so cute. I can't wait to tell him about the house when he wakes up. He's going to be so happy that he gets to stay here. Angela too. It's her house as well. I love her. She's changed so much, and Hunter has been happier since she's been back home.

I roll farther in the bed to move away from all the heat. Asher's sprawled out at my feet and Jace is beside me. He groans but doesn't wake up. *The hell?* Why are they all in Hunter's bed? I see Roman sleeping on the chair in the corner, and my heart breaks. He's so much better at touching, but he can't do it with everyone together. One day, he will. He's already doing so much more than I ever hoped for him.

I look over at him; his hair is so long now. I need to braid it again. But I sigh. He's a vision. He takes care of us when we all let loose. He's kinda the father figure of the group. He doesn't drink, so he drove us home last night. My head throbs and I groan.

Roman opens one eye and looks over at me. I smile. Of course, me making a sound wakes him. He shifts forward on the chair, and I want to go to him. I move around Asher. He's literally sleeping with his head hanging off the bed. I purse my lips to not laugh, because it looks so funny. I swing my leg out of the sheet and over the side of the bed, and as I try to stand on my tippy toes, my other leg gets caught in the sheet. I hop, trying to steady myself, but I'm not coordinated enough for that.

My knee gives out, I tumble, my shoulder hits the floor, and I'm caught up with one foot in the sheets. Roman's to me in an instant. He picks me up and looks down at where I'm tangled. He gets me free, and still, the guys don't wake. There's a snore from Asher, and then someone farts.

I snort and hold my hand over my mouth to stop

myself from laughing out loud. Roman whispers into my ear, "It's gotta be Jace. He had all those tacos last night."

I glance over at Jace. His face isn't as relaxed as the others, and then he shifts and farts again. I press my face to Roman's chest and giggle.

"Let's go have a shower."

I nod and let him carry me. Hot water will make me feel better.

"What do you mean, it's been sold? With everything? He can't do that. He can't sell my bed. That's my fucking bed," Hunter yells, and I can hear him from the living room, where I have been playing Mario Kart with Roman most the morning.

I drop my controller and stand up. Where is Hunter?

"Hunter?" I call out, and he comes storming into the room.

I know he's not mad at me, but he's fuming. Asher and Jace come down the stairs, wearing the same clothes as last night. Asher's rubbing his neck, and I feel bad I didn't reposition him when I got up.

"My dad sold the house last night while we were out," Hunter seethes. "With everything in it. All my shit has been sold to some asshole. I need a lawyer. He can't do that."

Hunter's so angry, but I wanted to tell them while they were all together. I wanted to tell him before this conversation. Shit.

"I'll fucking kill them." Roman's mad now. *Oh fuck.*

I put my hand up, but the four of them start plotting the new owner's demise. Those new owners, who just happen to be us.

"Hunter," I scream, and they all turn to me. Angela's in the room now too, and she freezes. "I didn't want you to find out this way, but... we're the assholes."

Hunter cocks his head and gives me a puzzled expression. "You spoke to my father too?"

What? "Hell no. Your father's dead to me. No, I wanted to tell you all that the asshole is me... us. Yesterday, I called Joe and asked him to put an offer on the house. He did. The house is all of ours. We own it and everything in it. Sorry, I just didn't want your dad taking anything. I love it the way it is."

"Mila." Angela's hand is at her throat, and I go to her, wrapping my arms around her.

"It's your house too. You will get half of what it was purchased for, and that's yours to keep. But I don't want you to move out. I want you to stay. This house belongs to all of us, and it's fully paid for. We don't have to worry about a thing."

She cries... I cry. Hell, we all cry.

"But where did you get the money?" she asks.

I point up and smile. "Malcolm. I inherited his money, but I gave it all up for Lillian."

Everyone just stands there, stock-still. Asher's mouth moves like he wants to speak but doesn't know what to say. I laugh.

"You mean, this whole time, our girlfriend was a millionaire?" Hunter asks, and I grin.

"Well, I was technically a billionaire, but only for a day."

"Did you... Wait up," Jace says. "*Billionaire.* You're saying Malcolm was a fucking billionaire, and you got all his money and gave it to your baby sister?"

I nod.

Roman grips his hair, and I wish I'd braided it now. I don't want him to pull it out. I love his hair. I grab his arm and pull it down, giving him my silent *stop* look.

"Gail and Joe put a little bit aside for college and a first house." I put my hands out and twirl. "First house. Done."

"But college?" Hunter asks and I nod.

"Well, if all goes to plan, Roman and I will be back at Ridgecrest for our senior year. If Joe is really a magician." Roman's eyes widen, and I hug him. "I know you're not big on the schoolwork, but we'll all help you. I just want you to be on the team one last year with the guys and go out with a win."

"Me too." Asher puts his hand up. "I told my

mom I want to transfer over. I was gonna surprise you on Monday morning when you saw me in red. But... surprise."

Hunter points at him, then they are chest to chest, and Asher grabs Hunter's throat. What the hell is going on?

"Fuck you, Asher," Hunter practically spits. "You're not taking my position on the team."

My eyes widen. "Really, Hunter?" I cross my arms over my chest. "That's the first thing you thought when Asher told us he transferred to our school so we can all go together? You're worried he's gonna take your position on the team?"

Honestly, from where I'm standing, it doesn't look like that's the problem. I think Hunter wants to kiss him, not hit him. And Asher looks like he wants Hunter to do just that.

"Hunter, apologize to Asher right now. That was extremely rude of you," Angela says, and it's her angry voice.

Hunter turns to Asher and mumbles an apology. I seriously need to get these two alone and naked and work this out.

Sooner rather than later.

CHAPTER 24
HUNTER

I can't believe Mila bought my house. Our house. All our names are on the deed like she said they would be.

Mom said she'll stay here until we want her to move. But she intends to travel the world with the money she got from the sale. First, she tried to give it to us, and Mila flat out refused.

And Joe's a fucking magician. Roman and Mila are back, and I can't wait for our senior year to really get started.

GO REBELS!

We might have a chance to win this year. Asher can fuck off if he thinks he's wide receiver. Jace has been training with him as a running back the past week since he said he's coming to Ridgecrest with us.

Emerson's our tight end, and there's no way we would replace him. Asher really needs to be a running back. He is built for it. *Hell*. Roman said he's thinking of going for wide receiver now that Sam has left for college, which is fine by me. I know I'm the best one on the team.

"Miss Mila," I say as she walks into the house. She pauses and eyes me warily. I just grin. "Come on through here." I take her by the crook of her arm and lead her to the living room, where the other three are waiting.

She stops when she sees them and narrows her eyes at me. I put my hands up. "Hey, I'm not the one with an M&M addiction. I had to stage an intervention before you turned into one." I tickle her and she laughs.

"Hey, it's not that bad," she defends herself.

And Asher cocks his head. "Really? You bit my finger last week when I tried to take one."

She puts her hands on her hips. "Now, wait up a minute. You didn't ask. You tried to steal one."

I laugh. This isn't why she's here, but fuck, I think she has a problem with her chocolate. And I need to get this over fast, because Jace brought his Christmas gift, and I'm kinda pissed at him over it. Because… it's better.

"Just sit your pretty ass down. We have gifts to give you."

She scrunches up her nose. "Gifts?"

I take off my hoodie to show her I'm wearing the *Property of Mila Hart* tee she gave me for

Christmas. The guys all do the same, and she gasps.

"Oh my god. Christmas?" she asks and sits on the floor beside one of the gifts. It's Asher's. He didn't tell me what it is. I asked a few times, trying to get it out of him, but nope. He wanted it to be a surprise.

"Mine first." Roman hands her a gift bag, and she looks inside and squeals.

She pulls out a black tee that says, *Property of Roman Valentine, Hunter West, Jace Montero, Asher Rossi.*

She instantly takes off the top she's wearing, and we all groan in unison as we see those beautiful tits. She slips it on with a huge grin. "Thank you, Roman. But isn't the order wrong?"

I'm confused, what order?

"It's the order of who fell in love with you first."

I shake my head and laugh. "Dude, if that's the case, Jace should be first," I point out.

"No, true love. Not just love, but that deep soul love."

"You never stopped loving me, Roman." She kisses him, and I get it now.

The order is correct. Roman loved her on another level. He always has, and that's why he waited for her to return. He never kissed another girl, even looked at them. He was waiting for his true love to return.

I fell hard for Mila when she returned. A love so

deep and pure, it snuck up on me when I wasn't expecting it.

Jace said he loved her, but I know he didn't truly fall for her until the stuff that went down with Grady. He saw pure love right there, and he was done for. That's why he fought it so hard.

And Asher... You could say him and Jace were neck and neck, really. He tried to fight it, but Mila's like a freight train. There's no getting out of the way with that hurtling toward you. He never stood a chance the day she walked into his life.

Asher gives her his gift. It's small, like mine, and I hope he listened when I said I was getting her a necklace. She pulls out a small box and opens it. We all move forward to see what's inside, and she chokes up.

Her hand goes to her throat as she looks up at him. "Asher, this is perfect." She pulls out a small chain, a bracelet. Attached to it are little butterflies. Five in total.

"Red, blue, purple, black, and turquoise." She looks at us all, and now I wonder what color I am.

"You're purple, Mila. I'm blue, Hunter is red, Roman is black—and yes, I asked him what his favorite color was before I bought it. And Jace said turquoise is his."

"You didn't ask me," I protest. He spoke to everyone but me.

His cheeks pinken, and I wonder what I said. But how did he guess my color was red?

"You wear red a lot. Especially your shoes, man. I'm sorry, am I wrong? I should have asked. I just assumed, and now I feel like a dick."

Mila's eyes widen and flick between us.

Fuck. "Yeah, mine is red. I just..." I have no idea. I didn't realize he noticed me that much.

He smiles and I nod. Fuck. My heart is doing that shit again when I'm around Asher and my cock wants me to touch him.

"Mine next." I hand Mila my gift.

Mila gasps as she opens the locket and sees all our faces. I got a photo of Asher when he was nine from Kate and did some photoshopping on my computer, and now he looks like he's always belonged.

I watch as the guys all lean in and smile. Asher's eyes meet mine, and I grin. Yeah... I got you in there too. He might not have been here from the start, but he sure as fuck was meant to be with us.

"I love it."

I love them all.

"Okay, Mila," I say. "Final gift."

She turns to Jace, and he looks toward the kitchen door, where James and Kate walk out with Mom, Madison right behind, and they have a box... a big box.

Jace couldn't afford his gift on his own, so they all contributed money for this very important gift.

As soon as James places it at her feet, Mila cries. "No, don't cry, baby girl. This is a happy time. We waited until you were more settled, and you can't cry. You need to open your gift."

I bring my phone out and start recording. She's going to want to watch this over and over.

She opens the bow on the box, and Madison can't contain herself. She squeals. Mila looks in and gasps, her hands flying to her mouth as if she can't believe it. Tears well up in her eyes as the little kitten meows up at her.

"Oh my god." She sobs as she reaches in to get her. She takes out the cute little white fluff ball and hugs it to her chest, sobbing and thanking everyone.

I'm more of a dog person, but I think this little thing is super cute.

"It's a Ragdoll," Jace tells her. "We went in together, and I ordered her. So, we had to wait longer to give you your gifts, since we were waiting for her to get old enough to come home."

"It's a girl?" Mila's up and hugging everyone. She comes to me and gives me a hug and kiss. "I love my necklace," she says, and I pat the little fluff ball in her arm. The poor thing is scared, as it's so little, but I know Mila will be the best cat mom.

"What are you going to name her?" I ask.

She looks down at the kitten, then grins as she strokes its fine fur. "Rebel."

James's laughter booms around the room, and I follow suit.

"That's a perfect name," Mom says, and Kate agrees.

Rebel the kitten.

CHAPTER 25
JACE

The bed is lined with rose petals. There are candles all around the room, and they give off a light lavender scent. I take a deep breath and go out to the living room to find Mila.

She beams when she sees me. The guys know the deal. Tonight's the night. I want it to be special. I want romance for her. After everything I've done to her in the past, I've been wanting to make up for it.

She forgave me. After everything I've done. She let me back into her life and into her heart, and I want to prove to her I will never break her heart again.

I hold my hand out to her, and she places hers in mine. I pull her from the couch, and she squeals as she flies into my chest.

"Hey there, sexy." I kiss her before she can say a

word, wrapping my arms around her waist and lifting her up.

"Have fun," Hunter calls to us, and I can feel Mila smile against my lips.

I drop her outside my room… Yes, this is my room. We all have one, and mine is closest to Mila's. I picked it right after she chose hers.

"Close your eyes," I tell her, and she scrunches up her face dramatically. I chuckle and turn her around to face the door. I peer over to make sure her eyes are shut, and I can see her peeking.

"Hey, no peeking." I put my hand over her eyes, but it covers half her face. She pokes her tongue out and licks me, and I just shake my head. Mila. I will never get enough of this girl.

As we shuffle into the room, I close the door, and it's perfect.

"Mila, open your eyes," I say as I take my hand away and place it on her shoulder.

Her head swings around, taking in the room. She sighs. "Jace, this is so romantic."

I grab her chin and pull her in for a kiss. "I love you, Miss Mila Hart. And tonight, I'm going to show you how much I love you." Her eyes widen, and I nod. "Yes, tonight, I want to make love to you."

I like control and I like it hard. So does Mila.

But I want tonight to be special.

I spin her in my arms and walk her back to the bed until the back of her legs hit the mattress and I push her. She lets out a small squeal as she falls back onto the bed.

"Jace, I have waited for this night for so long. I want to make love to you. I want this with you." She moves herself up the bed, over the petals, and lays there for me to follow.

I move between her legs and cover her with my body. I hug her and taste her lips. Slowly, I undress her, kissing every bare inch of skin along the way as she moans my name. She giggles as I get caught up in her bra.

"This one has more little clasps." She reaches behind her. "Now you get naked." She pulls on my tee.

I take off my tee and drop the shorts. She looks down at my hard cock as I give it a lazy stroke and puts up her thumb and forefinger an inch apart.

I grin down at her. "I'm gonna tickle you with my ant dick."

And Mila bursts out laughing. She wraps one of her legs around my ass and pulls me closer. My cock nestles between her legs, and I can feel how wet she is already. I rub my thumb down her slit until I find her clit. She arches her back and moans, grabbing her breast and working herself against my thumb.

I dip two fingers inside her and reach for her G-spot. The move makes her gasp as her pussy clenches around my fingers. I pull them out and suck them into my mouth, tasting her.

"Fuck, Jace," she whimpers, and I grin. I love when she says my name like that.

As my cock leaks pre-cum against her thigh, she reaches for me. "I'm ready Jace. I've been ready for a long time. Make love to me."

I pull away and look down at her glistening pussy. I grab the base of my cock and angle it at her, but first, I rub myself against her slit, getting myself wet for her. She grips my arm, and her foot is very demanding on my ass. She moans, biting her lower lip.

"I love you," I tell her as I slide my cock into her warm heat.

Fuck, she feels incredible. She pulls my face down, and I kiss her as I fully seat myself. I take my time kissing her. I don't think I will ever get enough of Mila's kisses. Her mouth, her tongue... just, everything about her.

But I can't sit here all night inside her without moving. I move slowly, in and out. She nudges me to go faster, so I speed up a little more.

"Jace, I love you, but for the love of god, can you go harder?"

I pull back slightly to see Mila's eyes and she's grinning. "I was working up to that. Slow then hard." I slam my hips into her, and she lets out the most beautiful sound.

"Yes, more. Please."

I slam into her again and again.

"Yes, yes. Faster."

She moans and I move faster.

I grip her thigh and roll my hips over her clit. She's getting closer and closer until I can feel her pussy grip me tight as she calls out my name, coming hard.

A shiver rolls down my back, and my balls tighten as I come. The orgasm rolls through me. Mila's stroking my face and whispering sweet words to me. I shudder, and my cock twitches as if it is ready for another round.

"That was so perfect," she whispers. "Was worth waiting for. Thank you, Jace."

I pull my cock from her, and she whimpers at the loss. I can't go another round. Not right now. I kiss her and head for the bathroom. She giggles as she watches me stroll out of the room naked with a semi. I go to the bathroom and get a washcloth for her and put it under warm water.

I return and clean her up. The rose petals are now all over the room and Mila. I shake them off and put her to bed. I blow out all the candles and slide in under the sheet and wrap my arm around her. She sighs as I hold her close to my chest.

"I love you," I whisper into her hair.

"I love you," she replies and drifts off to sleep.

It's not long before sleep takes me. And tonight, I sleep with a smile on my face.

CHAPTER 26
HUNTER

Our girl is ready for us.

Mila's laying in the middle of my bed, wearing a matching purple bra and panties. Fuck, she's gorgeous. Her blonde hair is splayed out on the pillows, and the way she arches her back at the sight of us has my cock jerking in my boxers.

Asher and I stand at the end of the bed and watch how she wiggles in anticipation. Touching her body, running her fingertips over her hard nipples as they peek through the lace.

"Come on, don't leave me waiting," she purrs, her fingers skating down her cleavage. Down her bare stomach and along the edge of the lace. She licks her lips and waits for us to move.

I don't move. I want to watch her... getting off on us. "You're fucking perfect, Mila. Have I told you that yet today?"

She bites her lower lip as her other hand trails down, pulling down the edge of her panties. She slowly drags them off her legs, never taking her eyes from us. I palm my cock behind the fabric. She knows what she's doing to us.

She throws the lace thong at us, but it lands short. Running her fingers along her leg to the apex of her thighs, she spreads her legs, and I moan at the sight of a pretty, pink pussy. She's wet already.

"Fuck," Asher groans beside me.

I look down and find him naked. He must have dropped the boxers while I'd been too busy watching our girl.

It's just the three of us tonight. Roman told us to explore the thing between Asher and me. I told Roman he didn't have to be left out, but he said I need to figure this thing out. The push and pull between us needs to be something we do with Mila, without him around. As much as he loves the group sessions, this is something he needs to sit out for.

Then he told me he was sleeping with her tonight... *alone*. Fair deal.

Mila sits up and looks at us. She smirks. "Kiss," she whispers into the almost silent room.

A simple word... Something Asher and I have done before, but normally Mila's kissing us too. It's not just us. My cock grows harder at the thought of kissing Asher. There's no denying it. I'm attracted to him.

He knew walking in here what tonight's about, so I don't overthink this. I move to him, grab his hair, and crush my mouth to his. He stills at first, and I worry I'm being too forward. I lick the seam of his lips, and he opens to me, grips the back of my neck, and presses his body against mine.

It's different than kissing Mila. His body is hard, and the stubble on his chin is rough, but it feels so right. Kissing Asher is everything. I open my eyes and look at Mila. She watches us, playing with her clit and making soft sounds.

I can't hold back any longer. I run my hand down his chest, down his abs, and his cock is hard. I run my finger along the trail of dark hair there until I grip the base of his cock. I wrap my fingers around it, and it feels good in my hand. *Different.* But good different. I wonder if he likes the same touches I do.

I pull away from his mouth and look into his eyes. I want to make sure I'm not going too far. That he's into this as much as I am. He licks his lips and gazes into my eyes. Heat and lust stare back at me, and my cock leaks pre-cum.

Fuck. That one look has me wanting to do everything I can to make Asher scream my name and come for me.

I stroke his cock, firm with a twist at the head, and his eyes roll back and he moans. I do it again, and Mila's breathing speeds up. She told us she would leave us to figure this out, but I didn't want her not to be involved. I want her to watch. I want her to get off as much as we do. Maybe in the future Asher and I will do things alone, but for now, I want her to be involved in all of this.

I drop to a knee and then the other until I'm looking up at Asher with his cock right there. I can lick it. My thumb drags up the vein on the underside of his cock. I hear the hitch in his breath as he puts his hand on my head. I smile to myself and move in closer, licking the underside of his cock, tracing the vein from base to head.

"Fuck, Hunter," he grunts.

I don't stop. I lick his balls, and he grips my head tighter. I suck one into my mouth and tug gently. I pull back and see the pre-cum on the head of his cock. My tongue darts out and licks it. I taste the saltiness of him and I moan.

Taking the head of his cock, I suck it into my mouth, taking him as deep as I can before pulling back and looking up at him. His eyes are hazy, and he sways a little.

He smirks down at me. "Suck my cock, Hunter," he demands, and I moan loudly this time.

I suck him in deep, hitting the back of my throat. My hand works the rest of him as I work him with my mouth. His hips thrust, and I let him take control. Both of his hands are on my head as he thrusts into my mouth, and I moan around him, taking him deeper with every thrust.

"Fuck, I'm coming."

He pulls back, but I chase after his cock. I want it. All of it. His cock jerks and his breath catches in his throat as the first taste of him hits the back of my throat and I swallow.

He pulls away and stares down at me. My first thought is he's going to be upset. I don't know why I thought that, but it's just so new, different, and I don't know what he wants. I just know I want to touch him and kiss him. This is all new to me too. I don't know when these feelings started; I just know that I don't want them to be one-sided.

He drops to his knees and kisses me, and I almost sag in relief as I return his kiss. I pull away and let out a deep breath.

"That was... I have no words," I tell him honestly.

Mila's head pops over the edge of the bed and she smiles down at both of us. "Hot. That was fucking hot."

We all laugh, and it's like a tremendous weight is lifted from my shoulders. My desire to taste him, suck his cock, has been in the back of my head for so long. Hell, if he lets me, I want to fuck him too. And I want all the same from him. So much so, I came prepared.

I jump up and grab the lube from my bedside

table and throw it on the bed. Asher eyes it and I hold my breath.

"We have to work up to that," he says, and I swallow and nod.

"That's okay. I just…" I don't finish my sentence. I jumped the gun here. *Fuck.* I'm fucking this whole thing up.

I feel a hard body press against my back. Asher wraps his arms around my chest and hugs me tight. He whispers in my ear, "I wanna fuck you. When I say we need to work up to it, that's what I mean. I'm not gonna take your virgin ass tonight. We will work up to it."

I hear the click of the lube lid and look over to see Mila grinning at me as she pours some into her hand. She smells it. It would be a funny sight, only that it says it's strawberry flavored, and I thought it might smell nice. It says it tastes like strawberries too, but I don't know if I want to taste it.

Asher pulls me so I'm standing at the edge of the bed. His hands lower to my waistband, and he slowly pulls down my boxers, freeing my hard cock. I don't touch it. God, it's so hard that I'm not going to last long at all. Mila reaches out with the lubed hand, stroking me, and it feels nice.

I moan, turning back to kiss Asher.

Mila works my cock, her hand so small and soft, and then I feel a larger hand, the skin rough from catching footballs all week, as Asher strokes me.

Mila's hand and his work me together, and I close my eyes and see stars. Then there's nothing. I open my eyes to see Mila's legs open and my cock nestled up against her pussy. Fuck, yes.

Asher pushes my back down, and I bend over her, kissing her as her hand guides my cock to her warm heat. I groan as I slide into her, the lube making everything so slippery as I bottom out. I pull out and thrust into her again, taking her nipple into my mouth and sucking. Asher's hand never leaves my back, and the other rubs over my ass, slowly dipping between my cheeks, getting closer and closer to that place I want touched so badly.

I hear the click of the lube again, and I don't turn around. I want this so desperately, but I don't want to get my hopes up. But as I feel the cool liquid run between my cheeks, I thrust harder, struggling to stop myself from coming.

His fingers dip down, and they probe at the place that's never been touched before. He's right in calling me a virgin. I've never even touched myself there.

"Relax," Asher says, and it's easy for him to say.

I'm nervous and excited at the same time. When his finger breaches me, I gasp. The feeling is strange. But good. I push myself back onto his finger, and he rubs a spot in there that has me thrusting wildly.

"Mila, shit." I look down at her, and she giggles. Her pussy tightens around me and my breath catches. *Fucking hell.*

"I guess you like that."

She looks back at Asher, and I nod. I do.

I thrust into her again, and he presses another finger inside, and this time it burns a little. But the pleasure hits me as he strokes that spot again, and I come undone.

"Fuck, I'm coming." I jerk and shiver as the most intense orgasm I've ever had runs through my body, all my nerve endings full of pleasure as I slump over Mila. I jerk a few more times and sigh into her shoulder.

"I… I… *Fuck.*"

"That's a first," Asher says, and when he pulls his fingers from me, I already miss them.

I kiss Mila and pull out. My cum leaks from her, and I rub my thumb over her clit. "Did you come? I'm so sorry."

In all this, we have left Mila without an orgasm, and that's unheard of. She shrugs, but Asher pushes me from her legs and his mouth dives down. He sucks her clit, and her back arches off the bed as she grips his hair. When his tongue dips into her, he's tasting me and her mixed, and I moan at the sight.

"Fuck. Fuck. Asher." Her body bows and she grabs him tightly as I watch her face.

I love watching her orgasm. Just watching the pure pleasure wash over her face has me growing hard again.

Asher pulls back and licks his lips. He has a funny smile on his lips, and he chuckles.

"Oh shit, the lube. Did it taste weird?" I ask him.

"Like a strawberry milkshake."

I will never be able to drink one of those again without thinking of this moment.

CHAPTER 27
MILA

'm in red and cheering from the stands and screaming out, "Go Rebels," with Sadie and Cadence in front of me waving a big Rebels flag.

My boys did it.

This is it. They made it. They just have to win this game, and the Rebels will be champions. They're already champions in my eyes. All four of them have worked so hard this year, training and practicing in the yard every day. You can tell it's paid off when you watch them play. It's like they all fell into sync and became a powerhouse... and I'm the girl behind them, loving and supporting them in their dreams.

Jace got his scholarship, so no matter the outcome of this game, he has a place. He actually has a few offers, but we've been trying to work out which one would be best for us all. Hunter was offered a scholarship, but he's not going to take it, since it's in Florida. Jace doesn't have an offer down there, and he's the one who wants to go all the way with football if he can.

I'm wearing my T-shirt that has all the guys' names on it. I don't care if anyone's judging me right now. They're the loves of my life, and I'm proud of them for getting here today.

"Go, Roman," I scream as he waves up at me.

His mom is sitting beside me. Angela officially adopted Roman, and he hasn't started to call her Mom yet, but she's working on him. I love this woman so much. It might just be a piece of paper, but I know the adoption means so much more to Roman.

"Go, Hunter."

He blows me a kiss, and Emerson does the same beside him. I reach out and catch the kiss and blow one back. Hunter sees Emerson mimicking him, and he shoves him. I laugh and wave to Em.

"Go, Asher and Jace," I call out, but they're not looking.

They're focused on the game and discussing something... probably the plays. Dad has been helping them out with their plays, even though he's still the assistant coach for the rival team. He helps them after school and stuff. But Lakeview didn't do well this year, with Asher gone and Walker off at college.

The whistle is blown and the game starts. I'm so

nervous, I think I'm going to throw up. I want this for them so bad.

The game starts, and Asher is tackled really hard. *Shit.* But he gets up and nods. He's okay. He's tough. The play commences, and then Jace throws the ball. It barrels down the field, and I hold my breath. He overshot it—there's no way—but Roman catches it and runs like I've never seen before.

Touchdown Rebels!

I swear I watch the rest of the game between my fingers as I keep hiding, so scared for them all. I don't want to see them disappointed after working so hard, especially these last few weeks. I've barely seen them.

Roman has two touchdowns and Asher has one. Come on, Hunter. It's your turn, babe. I cross my fingers and pray to the football gods that they win.

REBELS WIN!

Four years later.

"Jace, are you picking Lillian up from the airport?" I call out to him from upstairs in our master room. It has two king-size beds pushed together, and we all sleep in here most nights. Roman sleeps on the edge; he can't be in the middle, but he loves to fall asleep beside me. I'm so happy, my chest wants to explode.

"No, Hunter already left to get her. Said something about bribing her with candy."

I roll my eyes. That man. I swear to god, he always does this when she comes to stay. He wants to be her favorite brother-in-law. I said that's not how it works, but she's five.

We only just moved back after college. Angela bought a place of her own and has met someone. We like him very much. If we didn't, he would have four sons to deal with rather than just two.

Jace, unfortunately, blew out his knee freshman year. He changed his major and went into business with Hunter. I studied art and now paint watercolors. It's my passion. That and sketching tattoos for the shop.

Roman did buy the shop from Ronnie. Without any of our help. He worked hard and saved up then bought Ronnie out.

Jace and Hunter have started an online sneaker store, selling rare shoes. Hunter's collection started the whole thing off, and they have been doing amazing. The sales have more than doubled every month.

Asher went into robotics at Evansville. It was hard to pick the right college to suit everyone. But, thankfully, they had a great robotics program, and he's picked up a job in the city. It's a commute, but he says it's worth it. He loves the house and doesn't want us to move.

We're so happy here. People said there was no way we would last. That it can't work. But we have proved them wrong.

I pace the bathroom tiles and glance down at the test again. I'm late. We've talked about kids, but we were going to wait a few more years. Build the treehouse first, then start trying.

Oh my gosh… why's this thing taking so long? Am I pregnant or not? As soon as the result appears, I stand there and stare at it.

I take a photo of the test and send it in our group chat.

"We need to build the treehouse sooner."

GET BONUS

Want to see Mila and the guys build their treehouse?
Want to see Jace finally get in on the group fun?

Plus Baby fever!!!!

GET IT HERE

>>> www.authorbelleharper.com <<<

Are you wondering, but what about…

Grady?

Walker?

Alessandro?

Madison?

Emerson?

They all will get a chance to tell their story. Just join my newsletter or my Facebook group "Author Belle Harper's Readers" to keep up to date with my latest releases.

Thank you all so much for reading Rebels of Ridgecrest High and coming along on this journey with me.

Belle xx

BELLE'S BOOKS

REBELS OF RIDGECREST HIGH

Reverse Harem ~ Enemies to Lovers

The Pact

The Lie

The Game

The Win

OMEGAVERSE STANDALONE SERIES

Reverse Harem ~ Standalone

Harley

Storm ~ coming 2024

PARANORMAL REVERSE HAREM

NEW MOON SERIES ~LEXI~

Twice Bitten

Blood Moon

Rising Sun

FULL MOON SERIES ~ADA~

Fallen Wolf

Torn Mate

Shifting Sun

PACK KIBA NOVELS/NOVELLAS

Midnight Prince

Shadow Wolf

CONTEMPORARY STANDALONES

Naughty and Nice ~Christmas Novella

The Christmas Dunk ~ Coming November 2024

ABOUT THE AUTHOR

Belle is an Artist, Author, Wife and Mother.

She has an addiction to reading, notebooks, coloured pens and mint chocolate. She lives in the beautiful Australian bush, surrounded by wildlife and the smell of eucalyptus trees.

She also has a strong love for all 60's music, believes she was born in the wrong era and should have been at Woodstock.

If you would like to find out more about Belle, please come like and follow her:

Click Here to Like Belle's Facebook Page

Join Belle in her Facebook Group

Visit my website HERE

Sign up to my Newsletter to keep up to date with my new Releases, Free Books and Giveaways.

Sign Up HERE